NYX THE MYSTERIOUS

READ ALL THE BOOKS IN THE GODDESS GIRLS SERIES

Athena the Brain
Persephone the Phony
Aphrodite the Beauty
Artemis the Brave
Athena the Wise
Aphrodite the Diva
Artemis the Loyal
Medusa the Mean
Goddess Girls Super Special: The Girl Games
Pandora the Curious
Pheme the Gossip
Persephone the Daring
Cassandra the Lucky
Athena the Proud
Iris the Colorful
Aphrodite the Fair
Medusa the Rich
Amphitrite the Bubbly
Hestia the Invisible
Echo the Copycat
Calliope the Muse
Pallas the Pal

COMING SOON:

Medea the Enchantress

This book is a work of fiction. Any references to historical events, real people, or real places are used fictitiously. Other names, characters, places, and events are products of the authors' imagination, and any resemblance to actual events or places or persons, living or dead, is entirely coincidental.

ALADDIN

An imprint of Simon & Schuster Children's Publishing Division

1230 Avenue of the Americas, New York, New York 10020

First Aladdin hardcover edition April 2017

Also available in an Aladdin paperback edition.

Book designed by Karin Paprocki

The text of this book was set in Baskerville.

Manufactured in the United States of America 0317 FFG

2 4 6 8 10 9 7 5 3 1

Library of Congress Control Number 2017931425

ISBN 978-1-4814-7015-5 (hc)

ISBN 978-1-4814-7014-8 (pbk)

ISBN 978-1-4814-7016-2 (eBook)

NYX THE MYSTERIOUS

JOAN HOLUB & SUZANNE WILLIAMS

Aladdin

NEW YORK LONDON TORONTO SYDNEY NEW DELHI

To our mega-terrific readers!

McKay O. and Reese O., Natalia L., Madison W., Alejandra L., Amelia G., Maddie A., McKenna W., Micci S. and Brianna I., Caitlin R., Hannah R., Aurora DM., Lillia L., Ela N., Emily and Grondine Family, Kaylee S., Koko Y., Keny Y., The Andrade Family and Alba C., Sirena A., Kasidy Y., Derek H., Lorelai M., Brynn S., Lana W., Megan D., Aeryn B., Paris O., Tatiana T., Olivia H., Lori F., Kaitlyn W., Kiki V., Pinki S., Layla F., Laurie G., Caitlynn L., Thomas R. and Zoey R., Christine D-H and Khanya S., Ally M., Sabrina C., and Keyra M., Virginia Anna J., Shelby Lynn J., Samantha Grace J., Moira S., Elizabeth A., Abigail A., Caroline A., Kira L., Claire C., Ava Lee S., Sofia H., Madi T., Liliana G., and you!

—J. H. and S. W.

CONTENTS

NYX THE MYSTERIOUS

1 Night

NYX, THE TWELVE-YEAR-OLD GODDESS OF THE night, hovered high in the dark velvet sky in her horse-drawn chariot. With both arms, she began reeling in the starry blue-black cape that currently stretched overhead like an enormous canopy.

Darkness was giving way to the dawn of morning, and people on the ground far below were beginning to wake up. But it was Nyx's bedtime.

She let out a big yawn. After she finished her job here, she would normally go home and sleep the coming day away, awakening in the afternoon to hang out and do stuff. Then, toward evening, she'd fly back up in the sky to expand her cape and darken the heavens once more. However, this day was going to be totally different from usual. And she might not get any sleep at all!

As she continued to expertly tug at her cape and fold it smaller and smaller, Nyx spotted Eos, the rosy-fingered goddess of the dawn, entering the sky below.

Graceful as a dancer, Eos waved her arms, sending glistening rays of pink, purple, and orange to fan out along the horizon. The goddess, who Nyx figured was about her same age, wore a bright saffron-colored robe embroidered with lovely flowers. Which was pretty much the exact opposite of Nyx's outfit—a dark plum-colored gown studded with winking stars.

By now Nyx's expansive cape had magically shrunk to the size of a pillowcase. She gave it a few final folds to form a neat square no bigger than a sandwich, and then tucked the cape into the pocket of her gown. Picking up the reins of her chariot, she shot another quick peek at Eos and then looked away again before Eos could catch her watching. The two of them had never spoken, and Nyx sometimes wondered if Eos was afraid of her. Many people were.

Eos was sooo lucky. Because everyone loved the dawn, Nyx thought with a twinge of envy. Night, however? Not so much. It was kind of frustrating that mortals and immortals alike didn't understand or appreciate her as much as they did Eos. Just why the soothing darkness her cape provided should inspire fear in some was something she'd never understood.

To her, night was cozy . . . and necessary. It was a time of rest and renewal. A time to dream.

Simply thinking about sleep caused her to yawn again, even bigger. Her purple gaze flicked to Eos and she froze. Because this time, Eos's pale eyes were looking her way, too! The goddess of the dawn had caught her mid-yawn with her mouth wide open. Nyx quickly snapped it shut. How embarrassing!

For half a second, their eyes met. She had a weird feeling Eos was about to say hi or start a conversation or something. What if she made a friendly joke to Nyx about the yawn?

How would Nyx answer? She didn't know how to be funny back! Startled, Nyx quickly looked away and pretended to get busy with the reins. She always felt shy around people she didn't know well. Time to get out of here!

"Home, Erebus!" Nyx urged her horse quietly. As the colors of dawn replaced the night, he pulled her purple and gold star-studded chariot lower in the sky. Down, down, down they went.

No sooner did the horse's hooves touch the earth than . . . *crack!* The ground magically split open. Erebus skillfully sailed down through the crack and took Nyx and her chariot into Tartarus, the deepest place in the Underworld.

A mist-shrouded stone palace loomed on the misty path ahead. Her home. The moment her horse and chariot landed beside the black wrought-iron fence that surrounded the palace, Nyx leaped to stand in a patch of ground covered with fragrant star-shaped white flowers. They were called asphodel, and great fields of them grew in the Underworld, where little else would grow.

"Back in a few, Erebus," she murmured, giving her horse a quick hug.

Tiny blinking stars followed in her wake as she dashed through the wrought-iron gate, up the walkway, and through a polished ebony wood door. Inside the palace, her footsteps echoed across the black-tiled great room and down a hall. Within minutes, she burst into her favorite place in the whole castle—her bedroom!

She had painted its walls a lush midnight blue and studded its ceiling with white stars that could magically rearrange themselves into various constellations. It was so cool!

No one else had ever seen the room though. Because the only friends she had in the Underworld were either shades, aka the dead, aka human souls. Or else they were guys like Hypnos and Thanatos, the twin gods of sleep and death who helped check in newly deceased arrivals to the Underworld. Due to her nighttime job in the sky, it wasn't like she could ever have a sleepover even if she had friends her own age around here!

Zooming straight to her canopy bed, Nyx shoved open the heavy black brocade curtain that enclosed it. After pulling her folded square cape from her pocket, she dropped it into the travel bag she'd packed earlier and left atop her bedcovers. The bag was stuffed with a week's worth of clothes—pairs of black leggings, some black chitons, and her black cotton nightgown as well as makeup, money (though she wasn't sure she'd need that where she was going), and other belongings.

She yawned again. *Argh!* She had to shake off her tiredness. She had places to go and immortals to see!

Quickly, she grabbed the two papyrus scrolls—one an invitation and the other an essay—that lay on her bed by the bag. Though she had practically memorized both scrolls by now, she remained worried and confused by them. This is how the invitation went:

Dear Nyx,

We are writing to tell you
that we won an essay contest
celebrating an "unsung hero."
That is, a hero whose good deeds
aren't well-known enough to be
celebrated in any songs. And guess
what? Our essay was about you!
Principal Zeus said we could invite
you—our unsung hero—to visit
Mount Olympus Academy for a

WEEK, SO IMMORTALS CAN MEET YOU AND CELEBRATE YOUR GOOD DEEDS. WE HOPE YOU WILL COME! YOU CAN BRING YOUR CAPE AND DO YOUR JOB IN THE SKY EVERY NIGHT FROM HERE, NO PROBLEM, RIGHT?

SEE YOU ON SUNDAY! (HOPE, HOPE!)

THANKS, HERO!

—ATHENA AND ARTEMIS

Nyx could hardly believe that the two mega-awesome goddessgirls Athena and Artemis had written to her, much less that they considered her a hero! The essay they'd sent told of how, under cover of Nyx's darkness, the mortal Odysseus (a *definite* hero) was able to sneak home after the Trojan War and reclaim his estate. This was true, but it wasn't like Nyx had provided the darkness specifically to aid him. She'd simply been doing her job!

Night was a great concealer of actions. Another of its beauties was that it allowed what was done by day to be undone. Which was how, as Athena and Artemis's essay had noted, Odysseus's wife, Penelope, was able to thwart unwanted suitors. Thinking Odysseus dead in the war, they had hounded her to marry one of them. But she told them she first had to finish a special weaving. She worked on it every day. Then, while the suitors slept during the night Nyx brought forth, Penelope tricked them by undoing her work.

Here again, Nyx's nightly help had been merely accidental, though. Real heroes like Odysseus did great things on purpose. What if Zeus or other immortals at MOA realized she really *wasn't* a hero after they met her? Would Athena and Artemis soon regret their invitation?

Nyx poked the two scrolls into her bag. They were too long to fit, so she left the bag partly open with the scrolls sticking out of the top.

Her stomach fluttered uneasily. The moment she had both dreaded and looked forward to during the last few days had finally arrived. She was going to Mount Olympus Academy. Although she felt anxious, she was determined to show up. Because despite doubting whether she deserved to be called a hero, this could be her best chance of educating immortals about the importance of night and how little they had to fear from it (and from her)!

She grabbed her bag in one hand and dashed off. Reaching the palace entryway, she screeched to a halt and lifted a tall dome from a table with her free hand. About three feet tall and two feet wide, the dome had a handle on top and was draped with a cloth. Quickly she tied a cord around its middle to keep the cloth in place.

Minutes later, she was stowing her stuff in the back of her chariot. When that was done, she leaped in. Flicking her horse's reins, she shouted, "Onward to Mount Olympus!"

As the chariot lifted on a path that would take her out of the Underworld, she gazed up at the narrow slice of sky that showed through the crack in the earth overhead. She could just make out the last of the dawn's faint pink glow as it gave way to the blue sky of morning. Although pink wasn't at all *her*, it was the perfect color for the bright and pretty Eos, who probably would have fit right in at MOA. Better than Nyx, anyway.

Just before Erebus burst out of the Underworld, carrying her and her chariot with him, Nyx heard a flapping sound, like a flock of bats. Her horse must've heard it too because he bucked nervously. "Whoa, boy!" she soothed. After gaining control of him, she frowned and looked around.

Seeing nothing amiss, she flew on, never noticing the shadowy stowaways that had zoomed into the chariot as it rose up from Tartarus. After folding their wings, they slipped into the opening at the top of her bag and huddled together, as quiet as death itself.

2
Unsung Hero

EREBUS LANDED IN THE WHITE MARBLE courtyard of Mount Olympus Academy just before lunchtime. Grabbing the cloth-covered dome and her sparkly black bag, Nyx hopped down from her chariot.

"Thanks for flying me here, buddy," she said, patting her horse on the nose. "Cross your hooves Athena and Artemis aren't too disappointed when

they meet me." They might be, when they discovered how socially awkward a loner like her could be. Plus, she probably wasn't going to be the heroic type they expected!

Gazing into Erebus's big brown eyes, she snapped her fingers. *Poof!* At her command, both her horse and chariot magically disappeared in a burst of silver glitter.

As Nyx crossed the courtyard and then started up the granite steps that led to the Academy's front doors, she was aware of being stared at. Since it was Sunday, classes weren't in session. So instead of being inside, many students were out in the courtyard chatting with others, playing games, or sitting on benches to study. Their bright-colored chitons or tunics were in sharp contrast to Nyx's goth style of makeup and dress. With her pale face powder, dark eyeliner, purple lip gloss and eye shadow, plus her sparkly black fingernails, black velvet chiton, and black fishnet stockings, she looked and felt very out of place here.

She knew she should act cool and probably wave or casually say hi to a few of these immortals and mortals, but she was pretty rusty when it came to small talk or friendly overtures. Sometimes, when she felt anxious like this, a dark misty cloud would appear and swirl around her. Taking a deep breath, she calmed herself before that could happen now. The mist was a defense mechanism, but it would only draw more attention. She quickened her step and kept her head down, letting her long dark hair curtain her face.

Nyx found her way to MOA's main office without having to stop and ask for directions. When she pushed through the office door, the nine-headed lady behind the counter looked up. Her nine variously colored heads and Nyx's one head all did surprised double takes as they looked each other up and down. Although Nyx was accustomed to seeing the three-headed guard dog, Cerberus, in the Underworld, it wasn't every day she ran into a multiheaded person! And her goth appearance seemed to be just as surprising to this lady.

The office lady's yellow head seemed to recover quickest. "May I help you?" it asked in a cheerful voice.

Nyx set her stuff on the floor. "I'm Nyx," she announced. "Athena and Artemis are supposed to meet me here, but I'm a half hour early. I wasn't sure about the travel time between Tartarus and Mount Olympus," she babbled on. "My horse and chariot got me here faster than I thought they would."

"Tartarus?" Nine pairs of eyes bugged out in alarm. "That's the place in the Underworld that Typhon came from!"

Nyx nodded. "Um, yeah." It was true that Tartarus didn't have the best reputation as a place to be from. In fact, most saw it as the *worst* place in the Underworld. It was where the rottenest people ended up after they died. It was also where a giant creature named Typhon had been imprisoned for many years until he'd escaped to terrorize Mount Olympus not long ago. That probably made Tartarus seem very scary to this lady. However, Nyx found it perfectly comfy there. Especially since it was the *darkest* place in the Underworld!

Not knowing what else to say, Nyx shifted from one foot to the other and remained silent.

"Principal Zeus usually alerts me when new students are expected," the office lady's green head went on in a disapproving tone of voice. She began unrolling a scrollbook on her desk as if searching for some notation she'd overlooked about a goth-looking student coming to MOA.

The star and moon charms on Nyx's long, heavy silver necklace clinked against her sparkly black bag as she bent and grabbed the invitation. As she slid it across the counter, a voice piped up, saying, "She's a visitor, not a student."

Nyx turned to see that two goddessgirls had entered the office behind her. She had seen their pictures in *Teen Scrollazine* and *Greekly Weekly News* articles many times. The one with wavy brown hair and gray-blue eyes was Athena, well-known for being the brainiest student at MOA and also Zeus's daughter. The goddessgirl with the glossy black hair, who had a bow and quiver of arrows slung over her shoulder, had to be Artemis. She, along with her brother, Apollo, were champion archers.

"Welcome, Nyx!" the two goddessgirls chorused, coming closer. When neither of them seemed taken aback by the way she was dressed, Nyx relaxed a little.

"We saw you arrive in the courtyard a minute ago," said Athena.

"We were out on the sports field for Cheer practice," Artemis added.

Nyx frowned slightly. She had no idea what "Cheer" was, and she didn't want to ask since it might make her seem odd (or worse, *dumb*!). There was an awkward pause. Then, worried that the girls would think her unfriendly, she smiled at them.

They smiled back. "So, are you hungry?" Athena asked her.

Nyx nodded vigorously. She'd had nothing to eat except for two Hotter than Hades spicy nut snack bars she'd brought on her trip.

"Let's get lunch first, then," said Athena.

"Yeah, I'm starving," said Artemis. "Plus, we want to introduce you around. Everyone's dying to meet you."

Nyx perked up at the mention of *dying*. Living in Tartarus, she was surrounded by death and found it comforting and familiar. But before she could ask about these dying friends, Artemis corrected herself. "Well, not *literally* dying, of course. Most of the students here at MOA are immortals like Athena and me, who, you know, live forever." Stooping, she hefted Nyx's bag in one hand.

Before Athena could take charge of the dome, Nyx picked it up herself. The goddessgirls eyed her curiously, but they didn't get a chance to speak because the office lady interrupted before they could utter another word. "A minute, please, girls."

The lady held up the invitation and gestured (without touching it) to a blazing gold *Z* shaped like a thunderbolt that was embossed at the bottom of the letterscroll. When Nyx had first received the invitation she'd made the mistake of touching that gold *Z*. Immediately, a burst of electricity had buzzed her fingertip and she'd dropped the scroll. The office lady obviously knew better than to do that.

"I can see that this is official," she said. "But it's not like Principal Zeus to forget to tell me to expect visitors." Her pink head looked from one goddessgirl to the other. "So maybe you can fill me in on the details?"

"Sure, Ms. Hydra," Athena said patiently.

So *that* was the office lady's name. Nyx filed it away for later as Athena proceeded to explain why Nyx was there. Just as Athena's explanation wound to a close, Artemis gasped and dropped Nyx's bag. Startled, everyone whirled to look at her.

"Did you guys see that?" Artemis asked, backing away from the bag.

"See what?" Nyx, Athena, and Ms. Hydra chorused. Had Artemis been startled by a glimpse of her star-studded cape inside the bag? Nyx wondered.

"Some kind of shadowy thing just whooshed from that bag and out through the door!" Artemis blurted before Nyx could wonder further.

"Huh?" Nyx said in alarm. Ms. Hydra's heads all looked at one another uneasily as the three

goddessgirls ran to the door to peer both ways up and down the hall.

"I don't see anything unusual," Athena noted.

"Me neither." Nyx went over to her bag and peered inside it. It was still neatly packed and nothing seemed out of place. "Hmm. *Shades* are pale and wispy. But if any of them had tried to hitch a ride out of the Underworld with me, Cerberus would have sniffed them out and barred their way," she said to Artemis. "You must be imagining things."

Artemis shrugged. "If you say so."

Nyx frowned. "I'm not a liar."

At this Artemis and Athena exchanged a look. "Of course you aren't," Athena said soothingly. "No one thinks that."

Too late, Nyx realized her social blunder. She shouldn't have been so quick to assume she was being

criticized. If she wasn't more careful, Athena and Artemis were going to regret inviting her to MOA.

"Should we . . . um . . . let Zeus know I'm here before we go eat?" Nyx asked, trying to get back on the right foot by changing the subject. These girls seemed to view her positively, and she didn't want to mess that up. Plus, she wanted to meet Zeus. If she saw an opening, she would try to explain the importance of night to him. It was every bit as important as day! If only she could make him understand that, he would spread the word. Everyone would believe the King of the Gods!

Athena glanced over at a closed door across the way. "Is Dad in his office?" she asked Ms. Hydra.

All nine of Ms. Hydra's heads nodded. Her blue head clucked sympathetically. "Best not to disturb him right now. He's taking a little nap. You know how it is with the new baby and all."

"Athena has a new baby sister," Artemis murmured to Nyx.

Nyx nodded, having read this news in the *Greekly Weekly*. She was glad that Artemis didn't sound mad at her for her earlier remark about lying.

"One that doesn't sleep much at night," Athena confided to Nyx. Then she waved to the office lady. "Later, Ms. Hydra. We're off to the cafeteria!"

Hearing this, Nyx lifted both her bag and her dome before the other girls could offer. The three of them left the office. Out in the hall, Artemis continued on about the baby. "Yeah, thanks to little Hebe, Zeus and Hera aren't getting much sleep either. They're kind of beginning to look like shades themselves."

Athena nodded a bit worriedly. "I agree. They're looking very pale and tired lately." But then she smiled at Nyx. "When I took your invitation to my dad last Wednesday, he practically stamped that *Z* on it in his sleep."

"So, probably a good thing we didn't bother him just now," said Nyx. "Sounds like he needs rest."

"Right," said Athena. "Besides, waking him could put him in a bad mood."

Artemis grinned. "Athena's not the goddess of wisdom for nothing," she remarked to Nyx as they followed Athena out the door. "You know what they say: Let sleeping gods lie."

"I think you mean *dogs*, not . . . oh, wait . . . that was a joke, right?" said Nyx.

"Right," Athena said again. All three girls laughed.

Phew, thought Nyx. She'd escaped making another blunder. For now, anyway! As they made their way down the hall, she realized that she was already beginning to like these two goddessgirls. She hoped they liked her too.

Though her nervousness had eased some after meeting Athena and Artemis, it grew again when they approached the cafeteria. What kind of reception would she get from the students Athena and Artemis planned to introduce her to? Nyx worried. It would be easier if she was universally admired and appreciated. But she wasn't, of course. Not by a long shot. Fearing her veil of darkness, which many seemed to see as something mysterious and even *threatening*, the majority of gods, mortals, and beasts shied away from her. Well, if the others here at MOA would give her even half a chance, she'd get them to change their minds about her and the value of what she did!

3
Ruffled Feathers

NYX, ATHENA, AND ARTEMIS HAD JUST STEPPED into the cafeteria when they ran into a boy wearing a lion-skin cape about to exit. The lion's jaws fit his head like a helmet. Nyx gaped, suddenly feeling a little better. If people here accepted *his* "look," why would they have trouble with hers?

"Nyx, this is Heracles," Athena said. From the

gentle, sweet smile she gave the boy, Nyx guessed he was probably Athena's crush.

"Hmm." Heracles squinted at Nyx as if trying to remember something. Then his face lit up and he grinned at her. "Goddess of the night, right?"

"Yeah. Um . . . uh . . . nice to meet you," she mumbled awkwardly. Having lived a mostly solitary life, she wasn't used to social introductions, especially to boys.

The girls started into the cafeteria, but turned back when Heracles spoke again to Nyx. "Did you come by chariot? Want me to take it and your horses around to the stables for you?"

"Horse," said Nyx, nodding. "Just one. But Erebus doesn't need any care because he's enchanted. I only have to snap my fingers to make him and my chariot appear or disappear." She almost snapped her fingers in demonstration, but stopped herself just in time. "Oops. I guess the lunch lady wouldn't appreciate a horse and chariot magically appearing in here."

"Probably not," said Athena. When the others laughed, Nyx felt a little thrill. She'd accidentally said something funny!

"Could you take her bags up to the girls' dorm, though?" Athena asked Heracles. "You can put them inside the door."

To Nyx, Artemis explained, "Us girls stay up on the fourth floor. Boys' dorm is on the fifth. Technically, we're not allowed on each other's floors, but we all slip stuff just inside the dorm hall doors from time to time."

"Sure thing," Heracles told Athena. He took the bag and dome from Nyx, and Athena smiled at him

in thanks. "Later," he told the girls. Then he started to push out through the cafeteria door.

"Oh, be super careful with that dome! Its contents are . . . *fragile*," Nyx called over her shoulder to him. She had to speak loudly to be heard over all the voices in the cafeteria, plus the banging of trays and the clatter of cutlery. Her calling out drew some attention, and again she felt the curious stares of the MOA students already eating at tables around the large room.

Athena and Artemis gave Nyx a puzzled look as the door swung shut behind Heracles. "Fragile?" Artemis asked curiously as they moved toward the serving counter, took trays, and got in line.

"It's a birdcage," Nyx explained, following their lead and getting her own tray. "I brought my two parakeets with me from home."

When both goddessgirls raised their eyebrows, she added, "That's okay, isn't it?" Had she made yet another blunder in bringing her birds?

Athena shrugged as an eight-handed lunch lady used all of her hands at once to set bowls of a steaming meat and vegetable stew on each of the three girls' trays as well as on the trays of five other students in line ahead of them. The stew smelled really good. Hot and spicy. Just the way Nyx liked it.

"It's just that Dad has to approve all pets," Athena informed Nyx. "He's kind of allergic."

"A couple of little birds in a cage for one week shouldn't be a problem, though," said Artemis. "Oh, wait. We were going to have you sleep in my room. That might not work because I've got three dogs. They're kind of rambunctious, and I don't know how they'd be around your parakeets."

"She can just stay with Aphrodite instead," suggested Athena, referring to the goddessgirl of love and beauty.

"That should work," said Artemis as the girls left the serving area and started toward a table. "Aphrodite and I don't have roommates, so, like me, she has an extra bed," she told Nyx. But then Artemis frowned. "Oh, wait," she said to Athena. "What about Adonis?"

"That's the kitten that Aphrodite and our friend Persephone share," Athena explained when Nyx sent her a questioning look. "Luckily, Adonis should be with Persephone this week," she said.

Good thing, thought Nyx as she shifted her tray between her hands to better balance it. Birds and cats definitely did not mix! It appeared that despite Zeus's allergies, there were several pets at MOA.

"Sometimes I let Hypnos and Thanatos out to fly around a little, but they do mostly stay in their cage. Will that be okay with Aphrodite?" Nyx asked. Her question was forgotten though, as a girl with a flower tucked behind her ear and long red hair appeared beside them. It was Persephone herself, goddessgirl of spring and growing plants. She sometimes visited the Underworld, so Nyx recognized her immediately even though she had only ever seen her from afar.

Persephone sent Nyx a confused smile, but she didn't seem to care about Nyx's goth look any more than Athena and Artemis had. "Did I hear you talking about Hypnos and Thanatos being in a cage?" she asked.

"She was talking about her parakeets," said Artemis.

"Oh," said Persephone, looking less confused now. "I thought you meant—I mean, I know two men with those same names."

"Yeah, me too," said Nyx. "They're brothers."

"This is Nyx," added Athena. "Nyx, meet Persephone."

"Hi," Nyx said to the girl as they all went over to eat at the table Persephone had been sitting at before she came over. "I live in Tartarus," she added. "I've seen you around the Underworld with Hades." Hades, godboy of the Underworld, and this girl were each other's crushes!

"Oh," said Persephone, looking at her in sudden recognition. "Nyx! Yes, you're the goddess of the night. I can't believe we've never officially met. Next time you see me down there, you should give me a wave and come over to chat."

Nyx smiled at the invitation. "Sure, okay." She had always wanted to meet Persephone, but just wasn't the type to go up and introduce herself to people she didn't know. Normally, being pretty much a loner was fine with her. But it might be nice to talk with Persephone and some other girls her age every now and then. Like she was doing now!

"I named my parakeets after those Underworld guys—Hypnos and Thanatos," she said to Persephone as everyone tucked into their stew. "My birds argue a lot, so they remind me of those two."

Persephone laughed at this. "Hypnos and Thanatos are always fighting about which of them works the hardest," she explained to Athena and Artemis.

"Even so, they've always been nice to me," Nyx

said quickly. She didn't want these girls to think that she'd named her birds after the brothers to be mean. She was actually very fond of the birds *and* the brothers!

As her words died away, Nyx suddenly became aware that some kids at nearby tables were whispering and sneaking peeks at her. Her reception had been pretty great so far, so she was unprepared and embarrassed at all this attention. She felt the urge to flee—or at least to hide.

Uh-oh! Abruptly, the very thing she'd feared when she'd first arrived in the courtyard began to happen. She tried to concentrate on holding it back, but her shadowy defense mechanism kicked in anyway. An inky mist began to swirl around her. Within seconds, it spread over the entire room.

"Hey, who turned out the lights?" a boy joked.

But no one laughed. Even though the mist wasn't all *that* dark, Persephone, Artemis, and Athena seemed momentarily stunned by its appearance, and an apprehensive murmur ran through the cafeteria. Nyx couldn't really hear what people were saying, but she imagined it was along these lines: "Who's that weird girl?" "What's she doing at MOA?" "This mist is freaky!"

She was seriously considering ducking out of the cafeteria, when a beautiful girl in a pink chiton came up to the girls' table. She had long golden hair threaded with pink ribbons. Smiling at Nyx, she set down her food tray.

"Hi, Nyx! Welcome to MOA!" she called out, loud enough for the whole room to hear. "Artemis and Athena told me you'd be coming today. Ye gods! We're all so happy you came!" Pulling out the chair

next to Nyx's, she sat down. And just like that, the tension in the room eased and students went back to chatting with friends and eating.

Now that she was no longer the center of attention, Nyx's anxiety—along with her black mist—evaporated. She flicked a grateful glance at Aphrodite. "Thanks. Sorry about that mist. It happens sometimes."

Aphrodite smiled. "No problem."

"Yeah, magic can be unruly," Artemis agreed casually.

Relieved, Nyx ate another spoonful of her stew. "*Mmm,*" she said aloud. "This is delicious!"

Persephone smiled at her. "So you like Ms. Okto's Underworld stew?"

"*Underworld* stew? Yeah, it's cool!" Nyx enthused. Then she corrected herself. "I mean *hot*. *Deliciously*

hot!" She spooned up another bite as the other girls laughed.

"A little *too* hot for me," said Aphrodite, who was eating a salad. Between bites, she looked Nyx over as if sizing her and her fashion sense up. Finally, she said, "Your 'look' is awesome. I guess it makes sense that you'd like dark colors, being the goddess of night and all. But I've got a ton of clothes, so if you'd like to borrow anything, I could loan you something with a more vibrant dash of color just for fun. Maybe a pink scarf or belt?"

Before Nyx could think how to turn down Aphrodite's offer without seeming rude, a couple of girls from a neighboring table came over to meet her. "So you're Nyx?" said a girl with turquoise-colored hair. "I'm Amphitrite, and this is my roommate, Calliope." She nodded toward the girl beside her. The other girl had long wavy red hair similar in color to Persephone's. It was gathered in a loose ponytail at the back of her neck.

For a moment Calliope seemed at a loss for words. She was staring at Nyx as if she were some kind of mysterious and exotic flower. "Uh, hi," she said, smiling at last.

Nyx smiled back. "Hi." It was a small comfort to note that she wasn't the only one who experienced socially awkward moments!

Amphitrite glanced at her friend. "Calliope is a Muse," she said in an admiring tone. "She's inspired tons of artists, musicians, and authors."

"Including Homer," Athena added, after swallowing a gulp of nectar from a carton.

"The famous author? The one who wrote *The Odyssey*?" Nyx said in surprise. In his book, Homer

had written about Odysseus and Penelope, who in turn were mentioned in Athena and Artemis's Unsung Hero essay. So, in a way, Homer's book was at least partly responsible for Nyx being here at MOA.

"The very one," Athena confirmed. Her skin had begun to sparkle just a little more brightly after her drink. Nectar was what kept the gods and goddesses immortal. It also made their skin glitter, but it had no effect on mortals.

"So do you like being goddess of the night?" Calliope asked suddenly. "Seems like it would get lonely being out and about when everyone else is sleeping."

Hearing the question, the other girls turned toward Nyx to await her answer. Now was her chance to teach them a little about the importance of what she did. "I don't get lonely," she began. "I love being awake at night with the owls and the bats and other nocturnal animals. And the stars, too!"

She glanced quickly at Athena and Artemis. "It's true that night can provide cover for acts that aren't easily done by the light of day, like Odysseus sneaking home and Penelope undoing her daytime weaving. But its most important function is *restorative*." Her dark purple eyes flashed as she warmed to her subject. "You need sleep to stay healthy. And the darkness of night *promotes* sleep. Without it, your mood would be affected and you could become cranky, or even sick."

Just then the cafeteria intercom crackled to life. "Principal Zeus here," a voice blasted out. "This message is for Athena and Artemis. Report to the office. And bring your visitor." There was a brief pause, and then he added, "Now!" After some muffled thumping sounds, they heard him call out, "Ms. Hydra? Where's the switch to turn off this confounded thing?" She must have come to his aid, because a few seconds later there was a *click*, and then the intercom fell silent.

A new black mist began to swirl around Nyx as she became nervously aware that everyone was looking at her again. She did her best to brush it away with her hands and succeeded in calming it down before it spread. Athena and Artemis had jumped up from the table with their trays at Zeus's summons, so now she did the same. Luckily, she'd already finished most of her lunch.

"Good luck!" Aphrodite and Persephone trilled as Athena, Artemis, and Nyx headed for the tray return.

"Is Zeus mad? He sounded mad," said Nyx as they walked.

"I'm not sure," Athena replied. "You know what you were saying about lack of sleep affecting your mood? He *could* just be cranky because of my baby sister keeping him and Hera up at night."

"Yeah, and besides, he always talks loud like that," Artemis added.

Just as the girls passed a table where a bunch of godboys were eating, Nyx tripped over a dropped spoon. Her tray tipped and her empty nectar carton toppled from it to skitter behind a large column. "Oops. Catch up with you in a sec," she told Artemis and Athena as she went to pick it up.

The instant she stooped to grab her carton, she heard one of the boys at that table say to the others, "I bet Zeus is going to send that goth girl packing.

Unsung hero, my trident! What's so heroic about the night, anyway? Now, the sea—everything about that is heroic, tidal waves, coral reefs, sand castles."

"Yeah, but you really shouldn't have written your Unsung Hero essay about yourself," another godboy commented. "Because, as godboy of the sea, you don't qualify as unsung. Plenty of actual songs have been written about you by mortals!"

As Nyx straightened, heat as red-hot as the Underworld stew she'd just eaten crept up her neck and across her pale cheeks. Glancing over her shoulder as she hurried away, she saw that the speaker who had just dissed her was the turquoise-skinned Poseidon. She'd seen his picture in *Teen Scrollazine*, too. She didn't think he'd noticed her, thank goddess. That would have embarrassed them both!

Cheeks still burning, she hurried on to the tray

return before any of the boys at that table could look over and spot her. So she'd been right. Maybe Artemis, Athena and a few of their friends, and the teachers who'd judged the essays thought she was an unsung hero. But some people here apparently thought naming her a hero was a mistake. A feeling of doom and gloom came over her as she caught up to Artemis and Athena at the tray return.

A girl whose golden hair was streaked with blue was talking to them now. Her bangs were curled in the shape of question marks. Since her skin didn't glitter like that of the immortals, Nyx figured she must be a mortal. "This is my roommate, Pandora," Athena said as Nyx put her tray in the return.

Pandora's pale blue eyes sparkled with curiosity as she smiled at Nyx. "How come it's not night at

MOA now that you're here?" she asked right away. "And how exactly do you make it night?"

"I need to be wearing my special cape to bring night," Nyx explained as Pandora accompanied the girls out of the cafeteria.

Athena cocked her head. "I didn't know that!"

"Me neither," said Artemis.

"Can I see it?" Pandora asked excitedly. "Your cape, that is?"

"We're on our way to see my dad," Athena reminded her as they pushed out into the hall.

"Maybe later," Nyx told Pandora. Her cape was in her bag, anyway. Which should be upstairs in the dorm by now.

Pandora opened her mouth to speak again. However, just then a boy who looked a lot like

Artemis stuck his head out of the cafeteria door. "Want me to take your dogs for a walk in case you're in the office a while, Sis?"

"Thanks, Apollo," Artemis told him. "That would be great."

"Hey, Apollo, I've been meaning to ask you something. . . ." Pandora gave the girls a little wave as she followed Apollo back into the cafeteria.

As Nyx, Artemis, and Athena headed down the hall toward the office, Nyx wasn't at all surprised to recognize many of the Academy students they passed. She knew tons more about the gods and goddesses at MOA than they knew about her. Though Artemis and Athena had written an essay about her, even they really didn't understand what she did or how night worked. Despite her Poseidon-caused discomfort, this realization gave Nyx a renewed sense of gladness in coming here. She hoped Poseidon turned out to be wrong about Zeus sending "that goth girl" packing. If she could succeed in her goal of making everyone see just how important night was, this visit would be totally worth it!

4

Zeus

MS. HYDRA WAS SHUFFLING SOME FORMS behind the counter when Athena, Artemis, and Nyx entered the office. At once two of the assistant's heads looked up at the girls. "Principal Zeus is waiting for you," her gray head said briskly.

"He said to go right in," her yellow head added cheerfully.

"Thanks," said Athena. She took the lead as the

girls started toward Zeus's office, but when they reached the door, she halted. Looking over her shoulder at Ms. Hydra, she whispered, "What kind of mood is he in?"

Ms. Hydra's purple head popped up on its long neck. "Don't ask me," it said impatiently. "He's barely been out of his office this morning."

"He's just so tired, the poor dear," her blue head said sympathetically.

"Because of Hebe," her pink head added in a confidential tone. "Some babies just aren't very good sleepers."

The assistant's yellow head smiled at the girls. "But never fear. Things are bound to improve as Hebe grows older."

"Yes, but that might take a while," Artemis said. Looking at Athena and Nyx, she muttered, "In

the meantime we'd better be prepared for some crankiness."

"Crankiness is one thing," said Athena. "Getting zapped is another."

"Yeah." Remembering the buzz she'd felt after touching the blazing gold *Z* on her invitation, Nyx couldn't help wincing.

The girls pushed through the door without knocking, since Ms. Hydra had said to go right in. They saw straightaway that, except for a candle burning on his desk, Zeus's office was completely dark, with curtains drawn over its windows.

Zeus's big head was resting on top of his desk and he was . . . *snoring?* The only other sound in the room came from the bubbling, trickling waters of a tall two-tiered fountain behind the door they'd just entered through.

"Dad?" said Athena, tiptoeing closer to Zeus. But he didn't respond, unless you considered snoring a response.

As Nyx and Artemis followed Athena farther into the room, there were whispered exclamations of, *Oops! Ow! What was that?* Because the floor seemed to be littered with objects they all tripped over.

Once Nyx's eyes adjusted to the candlelit darkness she could make out a file cabinet lying on its side in the middle of the room like it had been knocked over by an earthquake. If there *had* been an earthquake sometime in the last few days, that might also explain the files, scrolls, maps, and board games scattered everywhere. Only there hadn't been an earthquake in Greece for years. So she could only conclude that Zeus was lousy at housekeeping, er, officekeeping.

Artemis stumbled over a half-empty bottle of something labeled Zeus Juice. "Ye gods. It's a mess in here again. I thought your dad had donated a bunch of his office stuff and cleaned up."

"Hebe," Athena whispered back, as if that explained it all. Which it probably did, Nyx figured. Babies apparently took up a lot of time and energy that might otherwise be used for cleaning. And sleeping. Now that she looked closer she also saw a lot of baby toys and baby stuff lying around.

"What do you think? Should we just leave?" Artemis asked softly. The three girls looked at one another.

"We *could* scribble a note to say we came by and—" Athena started to say. Before she could finish, however, Zeus let out a screech.

"Eeeek! Don't you dare kiss me, you slimy

Geryon!" The principal's massive head with its mane of wild red hair thrashed from side to side, but his eyes were still closed.

"He must be having a nightmare," whispered Nyx. She'd seen a Geryon once. They were dreadful one-headed, two-armed, three-bodied, four-winged, six-legged beasts with blazing red eyes, vicious talons, clawed hooves, and extremely bad breath.

It was exactly the kind of nightmare that Phobetor specialized in. He and his two brothers, Morpheus and Phantasus, were Oneiroi, the dark-winged spirits that caused dreams. Like Nyx, they also lived in Tartarus. Without ever leaving the Underworld, each night they shaped the dreams of mortals and gods alike.

Nyx had a soft spot for the Oneiroi. Whenever they happened to fly close enough to her palace to hear her birds singing, they were drawn to listen outside the windows. They would try to sing along, but they had no voices. They couldn't even speak. And their "singing" was just high-pitched squeals!

"Yuck! Get away from me!" Zeus cried out again. One of his fists shot up from beneath his desk as if to punch the monster out, but instead he knocked over the candle, which set some papers on top of his desk on fire.

Reacting quickly, Athena ran to the fountain, dipped out some water in her cupped palms, and doused the candle and papers with it. "Dad!" she called out, reaching across his desk to shake his shoulder. "Wake up!" In the meantime, Artemis raced to open the curtains and the windows to let in air and light.

The moment Artemis turned away from the

windows, a dark mist slipped out of the office through them. Nyx blinked. How had her defense mechanism drifted all the way over there without her noticing it had even materialized? Or . . . what if her coming to MOA was causing some weird atmospheric disturbance? She certainly hoped not!

When the sunlight hit Zeus's face, he woke with a start. "Wha? Theenie? Whatter you—" Glimpsing the other two girls beyond her, he jerked his head upright. He had a serious case of bedhead, and even his beard stuck out at odd angles. "Ahem," he said. "Guess I drifted off for a minute."

"You were having a nightmare," Athena informed him.

"Nightmare? Oh, yeah, I remember." He shivered. "It was so real and—" He broke off suddenly and glanced warily at Nyx, who was standing stock-still in the middle of the room. For a split second, the look he gave her made her wonder if he suspected *her* of causing his nightmare. But dreams were the Oneiroi's department. Was this something else she would need to educate everyone here about? On the other hand, it could simply be that Zeus feared her, as many others did. Yet why would this powerful King of the Gods and Ruler of the Heavens (among many other titles) be frightened of *her*?

"You . . . um . . . asked us to come?" Artemis prompted Zeus after a moment.

He yawned and then shook his head as if to clear it. Nyx couldn't help noticing the dark circles under his eyes. She knew how he felt. She had been up all night, so she was tired too! "Right," he said. "Take a seat."

Nyx glanced at the chairs around her. They

looked brand-new, with bright blue-and-gold-striped cushions. (Blue and gold were MOA's school colors.) Even so, there were big scorch marks on some of the cushions. Remembering the electrical spark she'd gotten from her invitation and not wanting to get zapped, she chose a chair as far from the principal's desk as possible.

Zeus yawned again and stretched his muscled arms high. Then he settled back in his huge golden throne. Focusing his gaze on Athena and Artemis, who had (more bravely, perhaps) taken chairs closer to his desk, he got right to the point. "It has come to my attention that Nyx is here to visit for a week."

Athena and Artemis nodded vigorously.

Zeus flicked a quick look at Nyx, and once again she sensed fear in his gaze. "The thing is," he went on, eyeing Athena and Artemis once more, "I never approved that visit. So I'm sorry, but she'll need to leave."

Nyx's heart clenched, but she said nothing in her defense. Athena piped up, though. "You *did* approve Nyx's visit, Dad," she said gently. "You've just forgotten because you've been so busy."

Remembering that the invitation was still in her pocket, Nyx pulled it out. Gathering her courage, she left her chair and went to set it on his desk. He seemed to recoil as she approached, especially when her shadow fell over the desk briefly. His reaction was just so strange. And a bit hurtful, too!

Zeus frowned at the invitation. He turned it this way and that in his big hands as if he suspected it might be counterfeit or something.

If he didn't want her here, maybe she should just go, thought Nyx. But she wanted to stay! If she didn't, she'd lose her opportunity to convince him that she and the night were good for everyone and were nothing to fear. If she couldn't get him to see that, what hope did she have of convincing anyone else?

"You were kind of distracted when you signed it," Athena said, nodding toward the invitation her dad held. "Maybe that's why you don't remember."

"You said whoever got the highest grade for their Unsung Hero essay could invite the subject of their essay to come here for a week," Artemis reminded him. "That was Athena and me."

A light came into Zeus's eyes then and he nodded. "Oh, yeah. I was going to judge those essays myself, but I passed them to a staff committee because I had too many other things to do."

Based on this remark as well as his reaction to her,

Nyx guessed he might have chosen a different essay if he'd been the judge. Maybe that was being unfair. Surely the quality of the essay, rather than the subject (*her*, in this case), counted most when choosing one essay over another. As for quality, Athena and Artemis "got" that she and night were beneficial. But they had missed some important things about their subject too, in her humble opinion. Maybe the other contest essays had missed even more things about their subjects, though.

Seeming to decide that the invitation was genuine, Zeus leaped from his throne and began to pace around his office. Now that he was upright, he looked even more intimidating than he had when sitting down. She judged him to be about seven feet tall! His arms were bulging with muscles, and wide, flat, golden bracelets encircled both of his wrists. She drew in her breath when she noticed his thunderbolt belt buckle. Happily, so far there'd been no thunderous zapping.

"I have to admit," he said as he paced, "my mind hasn't been in its usual tip-top condition lately." Coming upon the file cabinet, he lifted it as if it weighed no more than her parakeets' domed cage and placed it upright against a wall.

"Ms. Hydra mentioned that Hebe still isn't sleeping well," Athena sympathized as her eyes followed his movements.

He nodded and gestured toward the fountain bubbling away by his door. "After we had to put that Fountain of Youth into storage, I got this new one to replace it."

Nyx knew the story of Hebe's birth from the news, of course. Apparently, the baby had magically been born by appearing to Hera atop an enchanted Fountain of Youth, inside a big Lettuce Wrap. Though Hebe's birth story might seem strange, the births of immortals often were!

"The sound of the water helped Hebe to sleep every night for about a week. But then it stopped working." Zeus paused in his pacing and yawned, which caused Nyx to yawn this time, too.

Seeming to decide that their visit was over, he waved a hand in the direction of his office door. "Hera and I will find another way to help Hebe sleep eventually. Off to your classes, girls!" he announced before returning to his desk and plopping back down on his throne.

"We don't have classes today," Athena reminded him, still looking concerned about the Hebe situation. "It's Sunday," Artemis added.

“Oh, right,” Zeus said tiredly.

The girls all rose from their chairs anyway. “So it’s okay if Nyx stays?” Athena asked as they sidled toward the door.

“I did sign the invitation,” Zeus replied with another yawn. Already he’d lowered his head to his desktop again.

Nyx guessed that was as close as he was going to get to agreeing she could stay. Then she remembered her birds. Though she didn’t want to give Zeus a reason to take back his permission, neither did she want to lie to him by keeping her pets a secret. She turned to face him again as Athena reached to open the door. “I brought my two parakeets from home,” Nyx admitted. “Is that okay?”

“They’re in a cage,” Artemis added quickly.

Zeus didn’t even bother to raise his head. “Fine,”

he mumbled. Then he dropped off to sleep and immediately began to snore.

Phew, thought Nyx.

The three of them left the office and started up to the girls' dorm on the fourth floor. "I don't know why, but your dad seems uncomfortable around me," Nyx commented to Athena as they climbed the wide marble staircase.

Athena hesitated before replying. "Oh . . . you noticed."

Nyx's eyes rounded with hurt. But then Athena explained. "My dad's not afraid of much, but, well, he *is* scared of the dark. So, as goddess of the night, I guess you *would* make him a bit nervous."

Nyx bit her lower lip. "That's too bad. I'm sorry he feels that way."

"How he feels is hardly *your* fault," Athena said

reasonably. She grinned. "Hera told me once that he always sleeps with a night-light."

Athena and Artemis burst into giggles. Even though Nyx found this news kind of discouraging, she giggled a little too. Because the thought of Zeus, the strong and powerful King of the Gods, being so afraid of the dark that he had to sleep with a night-light was . . . well . . . *funny*.

They were still giggling when they glimpsed an orange-haired goddessgirl with small iridescent orange wings at her back above them on the stairs and heading down. "Shh," said Athena to the other two. "Not a word to Pheme about my dad's night-light, please."

"That's Pheme?" Nyx said interestedly. "I've read her gossip column in *Teen Scrollazine*."

"Exactly," said Artemis. "And Zeus's fear of the

dark is a piece of gossip Pheme wouldn't be able to resist sharing."

"Understood," Nyx said quickly. "I'll keep it secret."

Unfortunately, Pheme had unusually fine hearing and was now close enough to overhear the last part of what Nyx said. "You're Nyx, right? You'll keep *what* secret?" she asked as she came even with the three girls. Her brown eyes sparkled with interest as cloud letters puffed from her mouth and floated above her head to spell out the words she had said.

Nyx thought fast. "The secret that I'm a huge fan of your *Teen Scrollazine* column," she said. "I didn't want to embarrass you with my adoration."

Pheme's wings fluttered with pleasure. "Not a problem. I love adoration. So nice to know that I'm even being read in the Underworld."

"Yeah, we read your column *hot* off the presses," quipped Nyx. "*Super* hot, if you know what I mean."

The girls laughed. Wow, it was like they were all friends, joking around together, Nyx thought happily. This was probably normal stuff for these girls, but to her hanging out like this was amazingly and surprisingly *fun*. Maybe she wasn't as socially awkward as she'd thought. Maybe she'd only needed a little practice!

As Pheme continued downstairs, the other three girls went up. "Nice save," Athena said to Nyx when they were all safely past the goddessgirl of gossip.

Nyx beamed at her praise. "Thanks."

Even before they entered the fourth-floor hall, it was obvious that Heracles had brought Nyx's things up there and set them just inside the hall door.

"I hear birds," noted Artemis.

Sure enough, someone in the dorm had slipped

the cover off the domed cage and Nyx's parakeets were chirping up a storm. Several girls from the hall had gathered around to listen to the two birds, and now those girls peppered Nyx with questions about her parakeets.

"Hypnos is the blue-and-white one. The green-and-yellow one is Thanatos," she replied when asked about their names.

"Are they tame?" asked a girl with straight brown hair. She wore a cute wreath of ferns and berries atop her head.

Nyx nodded. "When they're out of their cage they'll perch on my finger or on top of my shoulders," she told the girl. "And they'll eat seed from the palm of my hand, too."

"Can you show us?" the curious Pandora asked eagerly.

Nyx glanced over at Athena and Artemis. "Okay to let them out for a while?"

"Sure, why not?" said Athena.

As soon as Nyx opened the door to their cage, her birds flew out. While they flitted up and down the hall, Nyx took the sack of seed she'd brought, out of her bag. She showed the girls how to hold some seed in their upturned palms, and they giggled with delight when Hypnos and Thanatos flew down to perch on their hands and eat.

The girls were in the midst of feeding the birds when suddenly, without warning, the hall door opened and Artemis's three dogs ran into the hallway. Because boys weren't allowed in the girls' dorm, Apollo had dropped them off without coming inside himself. He probably figured Artemis or one of the other girls living here would put the dogs in Artemis's room. Which normally would have been the case. Except the dogs spotted the birds right away. Before anyone could corral them, pandemonium broke out.

The birds squawked, dipping and diving, as the dogs chased after them, barking. Afraid the birds would be eaten, the girls screamed and ran after the dogs. "Stop that!" yelled Artemis. "Come back!" yelled Nyx.

Luckily, the birds could fly much higher than the dogs could jump. Eventually all three dogs were rounded up and Artemis shut them inside her room. Now that the show was over, most of the girls headed to their rooms. Meanwhile, Nyx and Athena coaxed the birds to land on their fingers and then put them back in their cage.

"Phew. Sorry about that," Artemis said to Nyx once all was well again.

"No, I'm sorry," Nyx insisted. "Down in the Underworld they're used to playing with Hades' three-headed dog, Cerberus. He looks scary, but he's really very gentle. And much less rambunctious than your dogs, which is why I guess my birds were so afraid. I'll keep them in their cage from now on."

All at once a big yawn came over her. "Excuse me," she said when she'd managed to close her mouth again.

"You must be tired after the long trip here," Athena said.

Nyx nodded. "Plus, I was up all night as usual. I only go to sleep when Eos, goddess of the dawn, takes over to bring morning."

"Then you should get to bed!" Athena exclaimed. "Let's go to Aphrodite's." Grabbing Nyx's bag and cage, she and Artemis pulled Nyx down the hall to a room. Since Athena's hands were full, she used her foot to knock at the door.

"Coming!" Aphrodite's voice called out. When the door opened, the girls all gasped. Because Aphrodite was holding a black-and-white kitten! It leaped from her arms toward the birds as soon as it saw them. Thinking fast, Athena held their cage higher. The cat missed it and dropped to the ground, landing on all fours.

"What's Adonis doing here?" Athena asked as Aphrodite swept the cat into her arms again. "I thought Persephone had him this week."

Aphrodite stayed in the hall but gently shut Adonis inside her room. "Persephone's mom decided to paint a few rooms in their house this week. So I'm keeping him out of harm's way and from possibly making a mess!"

"Rats," said Athena. "We were hoping Nyx could stay with you this week since you've got an extra bed. But she needs a place that's safe for her parakeets."

"Hmm," said Artemis. "Maybe Nyx could sleep in my room after all." She looked at Nyx. "I doubt my dogs would bother your birds if we put their cage someplace high. Want to try it and see?"

Nyx brightened. "Sounds like a plan."

They all trooped one door down. While Artemis held on to her dogs in her room, Nyx brought her birds in and placed their cage on a high shelf above a desk. She guessed it must be Artemis's "spare" one since the only thing on top of it was a half-dead plant. "Pretty," Nyx commented, stroking a withered leaf.

"Ha!" said Artemis. "Nice joke. Persephone gave me that plant, but I can't keep anything alive."

"Oh," said Nyx. She hadn't been joking, though.

She really did like the droopy plant. It reminded her of the plants around her home in Tartarus. Except for asphodel, hardly any vegetation lasted for long in the Underworld!

Athena had followed the other two girls into Artemis's room. She placed Nyx's black bag on top of Artemis's spare bed.

"Thanks," Nyx told her. Then she stifled another big yawn.

"See you guys at dinnertime?" Athena asked, moving past Artemis and her dogs to the door.

Nyx nodded tiredly. "Uh-huh."

After Athena left, Artemis introduced her dogs to Nyx. "The beagle is Amby, Nectar's my greyhound, and Suez is a bloodhound," she announced before letting go of them to see what they would do. Though they barked and leaped around at first, they soon calmed down when they realized the birds were out of reach even if they jumped up on the bed.

And after a few squawks of alarm, Hypnos and Thanatos seemed to figure out that the dogs couldn't bother them. They settled down to preen their feathers. Their cage was close enough to the window that sun shone through the bars, which was something they really liked. Soon the two parakeets were chirping away cheerfully.

Nyx gave them more seed and some water while Artemis fed her dogs. "Does your birds' singing keep you awake?" Artemis asked as her dogs gobbled down their kibble and then lapped up some water from a bowl on the floor.

"Nuh-uh," said Nyx. "Just the opposite. Their singing helps me sleep." She yawned again and then stretched. "Besides, I can cover the cage if I ever want them to quiet down."

Artemis laughed. "Maybe Zeus should try something like that with Hebe. Think a little tent over her bed might help her sleep?"

Nyx laughed with her. "Doubt it."

"Listen, I'm going to take my dogs out for another walk so they won't bother you," Artemis announced.

"That's so nice. Thanks," said Nyx. She yawned again. "Could you wake me up before dinner? I wouldn't want to accidentally oversleep. I have to do my job tonight!"

"You got it!" said Artemis.

After she and her dogs were gone, Nyx changed into the nightgown she'd brought from home and climbed into bed. It smelled like dog, and she supposed that Artemis's dogs slept there most nights.

Luckily strong smells didn't bother her. There were many strong smells in the Underworld, including sulfur, which smelled a bit like rotten eggs, actually.

Though not everyone at MOA had been welcoming, she was glad to be here. She hoped she'd be allowed to "shadow" Artemis and Athena in their classes during the week—their afternoon classes, anyway. She'd have to miss the morning ones in order to get at least *some* rest after performing her nightly job.

Closing her eyes, Nyx pulled the covers over her head since this bed didn't have heavy curtains around it to block out the light of day. The bed was comfy, though, and within minutes her parakeets' singing lulled her to sleep.

5
Reaching for the Stars

THAT EVENING, NYX WOKE UP WITH A START when something leaped onto her bed and stuck its nose in her face. "Down, Nectar!" Artemis scolded her greyhound.

"It's fine," said Nyx, sitting up. "After all, I've invaded their space!" As if they sensed her meaning, the other two dogs jumped up on her bed too. Amby the beagle rolled over on his back so Nyx could scratch his belly, while Suez the bloodhound curled up at the end of the bed.

"What time is it?" asked Nyx.

"Dinnertime!" Artemis went to the window. "Or about six fifteen, according to the sundial below."

"Yikes. I'd better get a move on!" After gently pushing the dogs aside, Nyx leaped from the bed. "I need to start the sun setting in just forty-five more minutes," she explained as she rummaged in her bag for one of the clean black chitons she'd packed. She quickly changed into one and then covered the birds' cage so they would sleep while she was gone. Then she dug in her bag again for her folded sandwich-size cape as well as a couple of Hotter than Hades spicy nut bars for snacks later on. After tucking all into the pockets of her chiton, she announced, "I'm ready."

While waiting for Nyx to get dressed, Artemis had sat at her desk and filed the tips of some arrows. Now she put the arrows back in her quiver and stood. "Great! Let's go eat!" Amby, Nectar, and Suez followed the girls out the door.

There were fewer stares than at lunchtime as Nyx walked into the cafeteria with Artemis and the dogs. Did this mean that some students at least were getting more used to her? She hoped so. She and Artemis got their food quickly. Aphrodite and Athena were waiting for them at their table, but Persephone had apparently gone home to help her mom paint.

Athena motioned for Nyx to sit beside her. "Did you sleep okay?" she asked politely.

"Yes, thanks," said Nyx as she set down her tray and took a seat. In a hurry to eat and be off, she quickly dug into the plate of pasta the eight-handed lunch lady had given her. Though it could have been spicier to suit her taste, it was still delicious. She shoveled it down while the other girls chatted about this and that.

All at once, Aphrodite, who was sitting opposite Nyx, leaned across the table. "I guess you don't get nectaroni and cheese down in the Underworld, huh?"

Nyx looked up from her plate. "Whah?"

"It's just that you're eating kind of fast, and Persephone told us once that food there is mostly toasted asphodel roots, so . . ." Aphrodite was making an "ick" face.

Here was another chance to educate. Nyx set down her fork, saying, "That's what shades eat. I tried them once. They're actually not bad." She paused a moment, then grinned. "Nectaroni *is* way better, though. Definitely. And Ms. Okto's Underworld stew is to *die* for in my humble opinion." She rose with her tray. "Wish I could stay longer to chat, but duty calls."

Artemis stood too. "Wait up. I want to see your horse and chariot." Leaving her half-eaten plate of nectaroni on the table, she added to Aphrodite and Athena, "Back in a few."

"Leave your tray," Athena told Nyx, after nodding to Artemis. "We'll take care of it."

"Thanks," said Nyx. "Later, then."

With the dogs at their heels, Nyx and Artemis sped outside to the courtyard. So as not to draw unwanted attention from the students lounging around on benches, Nyx said, "Why don't you show me the stables? I'll call my horse when we get there."

Once at the MOA stables, Nyx snapped her

fingers and Erebus instantly appeared in a swirl of silver glitter, already magically harnessed to her chariot. Artemis looked delighted and began petting the horse's muzzle. Before Nyx could climb aboard, the girls heard the flapping of wings overhead.

"There's Zeus!" said Artemis, pointing. "Coming back from somewhere on his horse, Pegasus." Stretching out its mighty golden wings, the flying white horse glided down for a landing a short distance away.

While Nyx was marveling at the beauty of the powerful winged horse, she heard crying. Zeus had a baby strapped to his chest, cuddled in some kind of comfy-looking cloth carrier. He dismounted and gazed at the infant in consternation as he led Pegasus toward the stable. "Hey, little Heebie Weebie. Why is it you fall asleep the minute we fly off on Pegasus, but the instant we land you wake up and cry? What is it you want?"

Despite her pink-faced wailing, Hebe was very cute, Nyx noted. She had bright blue eyes the same color as Zeus's, and her little face was framed by strawberry blond curls.

"I know!" Suddenly Zeus's eyes lit with an idea and he launched into singing a lullaby off-key.

"Rock-a-bye, Heebee
In the treetops . . ."

Artemis and Nyx dared to hold their ears since he wasn't looking their way. But amazingly, Hebe seemed to appreciate his singing. She immediately stopped crying and began to gurgle happily. For about two seconds. Then the wailing commenced again.

Zeus sighed. "You used to like my singing."

Nyx found it hard to believe that could possibly be true!

"Hi, Principal Zeus," Artemis called out when he came even with them. She had to practically shout to be heard over Hebe's wails.

"Hello, girls," Zeus replied.

Nyx cringed at the wary look he gave her as he opened Pegasus's stall door. Though she really needed to be off in her chariot, she decided to take a stab at getting him to see her as helpful rather than as someone to fear. When the baby took a breath between wails, she said quickly, "It must be rough when she cries like that."

Zeus gave her a small, tired smile as Pegasus calmly trotted inside his stall. "I don't know why she's so fussy. Seems like she cries at the least little thing. Makes Hera and me fussy too," he admitted. Then he yawned big. "We'd probably all feel better if we were getting more sleep."

Without thinking, Nyx blurted, "Maybe you'd like to borrow my parakeets for a few days? Their singing helps me sleep. Might help Hebe, too."

"Really?" Zeus perked up at the offer. "I've got allergies to some pets—cats, for instance. Not sure about birds, but at this point I'll try anything. I'll talk to Hera and have her get back to you."

While Zeus and Nyx had been talking, Artemis had taken it upon herself to feed and water Pegasus. "Much appreciated," Zeus told her when she came out of the horse's stall. After bidding the girls a good night, he strode off to the Academy with the still-wailing Hebe.

"Poor Zeus," said Artemis. "I guess it isn't easy

being the parent of a new baby, even if you *are* King of the Gods."

"Guess not," Nyx agreed. Hebe's fussiness had given her an opportunity, though. If she could help him out, Zeus's attitude toward her was sure to become more positive. And she'd be able to manage without her birds for a few days. She climbed into her chariot. "See you sometime tomorrow," she called to Artemis as she pulled her cape from her pocket. When she shook out the starry black cape, it began to expand immediately, even as she fastened its golden star-and-chain clasp around her neck.

"Cool cape!" Artemis said admiringly. With a wave, she was off to the MOA cafeteria again.

"Onward and upward!" Nyx shouted to her magical horse. Then they soared away to darken

the world and bring an end to the day's labors for immortals and mortals alike.

Far off in the west Nyx glimpsed the chariot of Helios the sun god. By now he would be almost to the land of the Hesperides, his westernmost destination. As his chariot sank lower in the sky, and Nyx's rose higher, the colors of the sunset appeared. Within the hour, Helios would descend into a golden cup that would carry him back to his palace in the East.

As Nyx's cape unfurled behind her, the deep yellow, orange, and red of the sunset darkened to violet and midnight blue and, finally, black. Nyx loved how the quiet settled over the world as nighttime took hold. Spotting some bats, she swooped low. "Hi, Squeaky. Hi, Flappy. Hi, Nightwing," she called out as they flitted around her chariot. She liked giving them names even though she couldn't really tell them apart.

As stars shook loose from her cape, they spread out hither and thither to their usual positions high in the sky. Her favorites were the Hyades, who had once been a sisterhood of nymphs. Every night they whispered their story to her, and though the story was mostly sad, they seemed content with their lot as stars. By now, of course, Nyx knew their tale by heart. Still, she never tired hearing of how, when the Hyades' brother, Hyas, was killed by a lion in a hunting accident, the sisters wept their grief until they were eventually changed into a cluster of stars.

Eventually, the time came for night to end. Nyx unfastened the golden star-and-chain clasp around her neck. With both hands she began to reel in her rapidly shrinking cape. As she was doing this, Eos appeared in her saffron robe to take over and bring forth the dawn. For a moment their eyes met. Again,

Nyx had a feeling that Eos wanted to speak. Did she want to be friends? Or was there some problem?

Suddenly, Nyx felt an awkward jerk on her cape. Her head whipped around. Oh no! One corner of the cape had drifted toward the ground and gotten tangled in a tall tree while her attention wandered! With all her might, she fought to free the cape, carefully pulling with one arm, then the other. If she tugged too hard her cape might rip!

Her heart was pounding and her muscles aching by the time her cape was free of the tree. By then Eos had moved off and the moment between them was lost. The sky brightened as Nyx finished folding up her cape and tiredly turned her chariot back to MOA. It was Monday morning.

After guiding Erebus in for a landing at the stable, Nyx climbed down from her chariot and gave him a hug. Then she looked him in the eye and snapped her fingers. As always, he and the chariot promptly disappeared in a glittery cloud. Pegasus's stall was empty, she noticed. So, even as early as it was, Zeus was probably already out and about on important business. Or maybe he had gone for another ride with Hebe, trying to calm her.

Nyx hurried to the Academy and upstairs to Artemis's room. She couldn't help noticing that the early risers she met along the way (who were presumably headed to breakfast before classes began), gave her a wide berth as they passed. Including some of the very same girls who had been so interested in her birds yesterday! What was up with that? For some reason, they looked as tired as she felt. Had they been up all night studying or something?

Artemis was already dressed and fixing her hair

when Nyx slipped inside the room. Amby, Nectar, and Suez were all on top of Nyx's bed. Though they raised their heads briefly and wagged their tails, they didn't jump down. Too comfy to move, Nyx guessed.

"Did you sleep okay while I was gone?" she asked Artemis.

"Not really," she replied as she swept her glossy black hair into a cute, simple twist high at the back of her head and then encircled it with a golden band.

"Oh?" Nyx tossed her sandwich-size cape into her bag and began to change into her black cotton nightgown.

"Nightmare," Artemis answered, giving no details. She whistled her dogs off Nyx's bed. "I'll walk them, and then they can go to breakfast and classes with me so you can rest in peace."

"Thanks." Resting in peace was a familiar phrase in the Underworld and it sounded super good to Nyx right now. "I'm sure I'll be up by lunch," she said as she climbed into bed. "I'd like to sit in on an afternoon class or two if that would be okay."

"You bet," the goddessgirl said with a yawn.

As soon as Artemis and her three hounds had left, Nyx got up again to take the cover off her birds' cage. Hypnos and Thanatos began to sing at once. After climbing back into the spare bed, which was still warm from the dogs lying on it, Nyx pulled the bedcovers over her head. Despite the shouts and laughter coming from the hallway as girls ventured out of their rooms to go downstairs to breakfast, she drifted off to sleep within seconds.

6

A Charmed Life?

"WHAH?" NYX WOKE UP AND BLINKED HER EYES in surprise when she heard a *whoosh* outside Artemis's open window. *Thump!* Something flew in and hit the floor. She got out of bed and found a notescroll addressed to her tied with a red ribbon lying on the rug. The words "To Nyx" were written on it.

"Guess one of those magical breezes I've heard about that delivers things to MOA brought you?"

she asked as she picked it up. Of course, the scroll didn't answer. She untied its ribbon and unrolled it. *Meet us outside in the marble courtyard at one o'clock*, the note said. Artemis's signature was at the bottom. She hadn't said who "us" was, but Nyx figured the goddessgirl meant her and her BFFs. Or maybe her and her dogs?

She looked out the window. According to the sundial below, it was twelve thirty already. She needed to get going! After a quick shower in the bathroom that Artemis had shown her down the hall, she tended to her birds. They'd been twittering at each other, as if deep in a private conversation since she'd awakened. Now Hypnos began fluffing out his feathers and fluttering around the cage.

"Want to fly free for a bit?" she asked him. "No dogs around now, so what could it hurt?" After closing the window, she opened the cage door. At first the birds just remained inside and flew to the top of their cage, landing on the swing that dangled from a hook there. "Come on out. Have fun! Explore!" she urged as she put fresh seed and water inside their cage.

Finally, with loud squawks, Hypnos and Thanatos spread their wings and zoomed out. They began flying laps around the room, stopping now and then to perch on top of a wardrobe or at the foot of a bed or on the windowsill.

Nyx gathered up the top layer of a stack of papyrus sheets she'd laid at the bottom of her parakeets' cage to catch spilled seed and the birds' droppings. As she dumped the sheets in the woven trash basket under Artemis's desk, she noticed that some of the papyrus had been torn up and chewed. That was unusual.

"You guys feeling stressed out?" she asked her birds. "Too much travel yesterday? Anxiety over Artemis's dogs?" She supposed it was possible. "Well, we'll be home before too long," she assured them.

When she was ready to leave at last, she coaxed both birds to land on her upturned palm. Then, holding the gate of their cage open, she gently slid her hand with the birds halfway inside. After they hopped off, she shut the gate, carefully latched it, and reopened the room's window to let in fresh air.

"Be good," she told them jokingly before she went downstairs to meet Artemis and whoever else "us" included.

It was a beautifully warm and sunny day at Mount Olympus. Turned out that Artemis, her dogs, *and* her three BFFs were all waiting at the bottom of the granite steps that led from the Academy's front

doors to the marble courtyard below. As soon as the girls saw Nyx, they waved her closer.

"We thought we'd all have a picnic for lunch," Artemis told her, pointing to lidded baskets (presumably filled with food) that Aphrodite and Athena were holding.

"After all, it's such a nice day," Persephone added cheerfully. She had a flower-patterned blanket tucked under her arm, which Nyx guessed she'd brought for everyone to sit on.

"Sounds fun," Nyx said. She'd only ever been to one picnic before. It had been held in the Elysian Fields, the Underworld's most desirable neighborhood. The shades who were lucky enough to get sent there got to feast, play, and sing forevermore.

Leaving the courtyard, the girls walked toward the sports fields beyond the Academy. Amby, Nectar, and Suez ran on ahead, pausing now and then to sniff at some interesting smell or to roll in the grass.

Artemis stopped near a fantastic fountain featuring several golden dolphins. Water spouted from their mouths to fall into a wide pool at the base of the fountain. "How about here?" she asked.

"Perfect." Persephone shook out the blanket she'd brought, then laid it on the grass near the short stone wall that bordered the fountain. After the girls all got comfy on the blanket, Athena and Aphrodite unpacked the baskets and handed around the hero sandwiches, apples, chips, and Oracle-O cookies they'd brought from the cafeteria.

As they munched on the picnic foods, Athena asked Nyx, "So how did it go last night?"

Nyx noticed that everyone seemed to pause in their eating to await her reply. As usual, it made her

uncomfortable to be the center of attention. "Fine," she said at last.

Aphrodite arched an eyebrow. "Details, please. We know what you do, but would really like to hear how it actually works—that is, if it's not a secret or anything."

"It's not. And, sure, I'll tell you," said Nyx. Before her anxiety could take hold and a dark mist swirl around her, she launched into an explanation. Because this was another opportunity to educate these girls about her life as goddess of the night!

"So here's how it goes. First, I put on my magic cape. Then my horse, Erebus, pulls my chariot up and away. As we fly higher, the cape expands behind me across the sky, turning it dark and shaking off stars, too."

"Cool!" Persephone enthused. Then she yawned.

Did her job sound boring? Nyx immediately worried. *She* didn't think it was. Even if it was the same routine night after night. However, she was used to a life that was much quieter than the life these girls lived.

"So does anything unusual ever happen? Thunderstorms, hail, stuff like that?" Artemis asked, reaching for a handful of chips.

"Well, the weather can be troublesome at times, but I like that it's never the same. And sometimes creatures come along. Some bats came out last night." Nyx smiled at the recollection. "I named them Squeaky, Flappy, and Nightwing."

She stopped speaking and took another bite of her sandwich. No one said a word. It was as if the other girls were waiting for the rest of the story. But there *wasn't* any "rest of the story." She guessed she could tell about how her cape had gotten tangled. That had been kind of exciting, but it seemed a bad reflection on her abilities. She wished someone else would speak and finally someone did.

"Medusa has names for all her snakes," Persephone piped up brightly.

"The snakey-haired girl? I've seen her around the school," Nyx said, glad to make someone else the topic of conversation. Just yesterday she'd worried about others seeing her as too mysterious and exotic to fit in, but now she was more worried about seeming too *dull*. She'd always thought of her life as a charmed one, feeling lucky to do what she did. But maybe she simply thought that because this was the only way of living she'd ever known. The lonely life she saw reflected back to her through these girls' eyes was making her think differently.

To keep the focus off her—and because she was truly curious about the day-to-day lives of these goddessgirls—she began to ask *them* questions. *Which MOA classes are the most fun? What do you guys do in your spare time (besides having picnics!)? What are godboys like and which are the coolest?*

In addition to funny details about the boys (like that Poseidon played with tubby toys and wore flippers in the bathtub!), the girls told her about their classes (Hero-ology was a favorite, except Aphrodite preferred Beauty-ology). It seemed they often shopped at the Immortal Marketplace, sipped shakes with friends at the Supernatural Market, and took special trips to concerts and amusement parks. Once, they'd even gone to Egypt!

"Wow, that all sounds amazing!" Nyx exclaimed. Even though she knew she was a loner at heart, she

found herself longing to be a bit more like these other goddesses. To be outgoing and . . . well . . . *carefree*. Because, she realized now, her life was anything *but* that. Unlike these other girls, she had a routine job with big responsibilities. Taking even a single night off was not an option.

Toward the end of lunch, some boys began playing soccer in the field below the girls. Suddenly, an errant kick sent a ball flying their way. "Duck!" yelled one of the boys. Confused, Nyx looked up in the sky for a quacking bird and got beaned in the head.

"Ow!" Startled, she was unable to control the black mist that began to spiral around them and their picnic.

"Whoa!" said Apollo, who'd come after the ball. He skidded to a stop before Nyx. "Sorry about that. You okay?" he asked, peering at her through the mist.

Embarrassed more than hurt (Duh! He'd meant duck as a *verb*, not an animal!), Nyx waved away the mist. "I'm fine. It's just a reaction that sometimes happens when I'm startled or anxious. Like how some people's faces turn red when they get embarrassed."

"Weird," Apollo said, scooping up the ball.

Nyx frowned. She didn't want to be weird. Or exotic. And not dull, either. She just wanted to be herself!

Yawning, Apollo tossed the ball from one hand to the other, whirled it around his back, and then twirled it on one finger. When it fell off the finger, he chased it as it rolled to a stop beneath the fountain.

"Whoa!" he said, scooping up the ball. "I'm off my game today. I had this horrible dream last night that a giant scorpion was chasing me in the Forest of the Beasts. Woke me up way too early and then I couldn't get back to sleep."

"The Forest of the Beasts is a place down on Earth where Beast-ology classes go once a month," Artemis explained to Nyx. "We practice defending ourselves against simulated monsters that our teacher, Professor Ladon, creates."

"Yeah, only there was nothing 'simulated' about the scorpion in my dream," Apollo told them. "It had these enormous crablike claws and eight hairy legs, and it was about to strike me with its venomous tail when I screamed and woke up."

"Sounds horrifying," Athena commiserated. Then, just like Apollo had done, she yawned too. "I didn't sleep well last night, either."

With her hand covering her mouth, Aphrodite yawned too. "Me neither. I only got about half of my usual beauty sleep."

"Stop yawning, everyone," Artemis said. "It's catching!" Then she yawned too.

Talk about *weird*! thought Nyx. Why would these immortals all toss and turn the very same night? Could her powers somehow be affecting them during the day in a way that later disrupted their sleep at night?

"Anyway, glad you're okay," Apollo said to Nyx. Then, grinning crookedly, he ran off with the ball.

Ping! Ping! Ping! The lyrebell sounded a warning that fourth-period classes would soon begin. The girls gathered up the remains of their picnic and started back to the Academy.

"Artemis and I have Beauty-ology this period," Aphrodite said to Nyx on the way in. "Want to come with us? Today is Makeup Monday, and that

means we can use our class time to experiment with makeup or to *make up* missing assignments. Hey! We could give you a makeover!"

Artemis rolled her eyes. "Nyx looks fine the way she is."

Nyx sent her a smile, grateful for the comment. Still, she hesitated. She'd always liked her "look" too, but now she found herself wondering if a different look might make her seem less weird (or dull!) to MOA students. It wouldn't be permanent, just for a little while. She could go back to her usual look when she left MOA to return to the Underworld. So what did she have to lose?

"Okay, it'll be fun to hang out and do makeup," she told Aphrodite. "Let's go!"

7
A New Look

APHRODITE AND ARTEMIS INTRODUCED NYX TO the Beauty-ology teacher, Ms. ThreeGraces, as soon as the girls, trailed by Artemis's dogs, entered the classroom. The impeccably groomed teacher's hair, chiton, and makeup were as perfect as in a painting. Her eyes swept over Nyx's goth appearance with interest, but not disapproval, Nyx was pleased to note.

"Welcome, Nyx," Ms. ThreeGraces said in elegant, soothing tones. She smiled warmly. "I hope you're enjoying your stay here at MOA. Please feel free to look around the classroom and take part in any activities you'd like."

As accepting as the teacher was toward Nyx, she was not as happy to see Artemis's dogs, however. "Dogs and makeup don't mix," she told Artemis firmly. "You may be excused for a few minutes to take them up to your room."

After Artemis and her dogs left, Nyx had a moment of anxiety. Would her birds be safe all alone with the dogs? Luckily, she was able to dismiss her nervousness before her black shadowy mist could swirl around her. The birds were safely inside their cage on top of a high shelf, she reminded herself. The dogs had grown used to them by now and

would surely just curl up on her . . . er . . . *their* bed to nap.

Aphrodite linked her arm through Nyx's. "The cosmetology area is over here," she said, steering Nyx to a group of tables in one corner of the room. Scattered across the tables were several boxes of tissues, and maybe a dozen bronze mirrors. Nyx hid a smile when she noticed Aphrodite leaning over one of them to admire her own reflection. While not exactly vain, Aphrodite definitely liked to look good. But then, she was the goddessgirl of beauty!

"Have a seat," Aphrodite said, motioning to a chair at one of the tables. "Artemis won't mind if we get started before she's back. In the meantime, I'll get the things we'll need." So saying, she stepped over to some nearby shelves that were stacked with various supplies, including life-size fake heads.

Aphrodite scanned the shelves with a practiced eye and selected several boxes and jars. These she deposited atop the table in front of Nyx. Then she went back to the shelves for a few more items.

One of the boxes was jiggling. When Nyx opened it to see what was inside, a magic makeup brush catapulted out. Immediately, it flew up till it was level with her nose, about a foot away. Hovering in midair, its bristles curved into a question-mark shape as it contemplated her face.

"I guess you're thinking you've got your work cut out for you, huh?" joked Nyx.

Overhearing as she returned with a handful of lip glosses, Aphrodite laughed. "No, it's just waiting for instructions." As she set down the lip glosses, which were in varying shades of pink, red, and orange—colors Nyx *never* wore—Aphrodite said to the makeup brush, “Be patient. We’re not quite ready for your help yet.”

For a second or two the brush seemed to slump with disappointment, but then it flew down to rest on top of its box until needed.

Aphrodite handed Nyx a small pot of cream and a couple of tissues. “Makeup remover,” she told Nyx. “First step is to get rid of the white face powder and all that black eyeliner. Oh, and your purple lip gloss too.” Glancing down at Nyx’s fingernails as Nyx reached for the tissues, Aphrodite added, “We’ll deal with the nail polish later.”

“Okay,” said Nyx. However, despite her consent to the makeover, she was starting to feel apprehensive. Her hands shook a little as she spread the cream all over her face, but at least her nervousness didn’t trigger the black mist. She had just finished

wiping the cream off with the tissues when Artemis returned.

"I like it!" she exclaimed, peering at Nyx's face. Then she smiled at Aphrodite. "That's a great look for her!"

Aphrodite rolled her eyes. "She's only just removed her *old* makeup. We haven't yet started with the new."

"Oh." Artemis grinned at Nyx. "Then I guess that means you're a natural beauty. Or, given that you're a goddess, a *super*natural beauty!"

Surprised at the compliment, Nyx mumbled, "Uh . . . thanks." No one remarked on her looks in the Underworld. Beauty was mostly a concern of the living, not the dead.

"Artemis is right," Aphrodite agreed, eyeing Nyx's face in a professional way. "A bare minimum

of makeup is all you'll need. We won't use any concealer or face powder because your skin is flawless."

Hurrah! thought Nyx. She'd have less to wash off if she didn't like the results.

First Aphrodite and Artemis surveyed the range of eye shadows that Aphrodite had brought and debated which to use. Hearing them, other girls in the class wandered over to add their opinions. Every now and then some of that same wariness she'd seen in students upon her return to MOA this morning crept into their eyes. But mostly they seemed to forget that she was the goddess of night. Maybe because she looked so unlike herself now?

Eventually, the group settled unanimously on a sparkly blue eye shadow—almost a midnight blue—that Nyx actually liked too. Excited to have work to do, the makeup brush sprang up from its box when

Aphrodite called to it. Then it happily whisked the blue powder across Nyx's eyelids.

"Nice work," Aphrodite told it when it had finished. Nyx opened her eyes in time to see the brush curve its bristle tips in a little bow. Then it flipped end over end to land in its box again. The lid shut tight behind it.

Now Aphrodite opened a box containing a new brush with fewer bristles, and called on it to apply eyeliner. "Just a thin line along her upper eyelashes," she instructed. Immediately, the brush dipped itself into a pot of black makeup. Nyx leaned back her head and closed her eyes again so the brush could do its work. She only felt a gentle flutter across her eyelids as it swept liner from the inside corner of each eye to the outside.

"You have great eyelashes—so long and thick,"

Aphrodite remarked as yet another brush applied a small amount of mascara to Nyx's lashes. Once this task was completed, Aphrodite nodded her approval of the result. "And now for lip gloss." Again the girls all offered suggestions. Everyone agreed on red, but half voted for an orangey-red called "Dragon Fire" while the other half favored a darker red called "Ruby Wine."

Aphrodite held both lip glosses up to Nyx's face. "Ruby Wine," she said decisively. And that was that. Because Aphrodite was MOA's reigning (though unofficial) queen of fashion!

A matching dark red polish was found for Nyx's nails. Two volunteers quickly removed the old black polish and repainted her nails with the new polish.

In the end, the girls all stood back, looking delighted with the result of the makeover. "She

looks . . . *normal* now," Nyx heard one girl whisper to another.

Normalcy. Yes! That was exactly what Nyx was hoping to experience. Briefly, anyway. However, when she looked at herself in one of the bronze mirrors, she couldn't help gulping. Oh, she looked beautiful, she supposed, in an MOA kind of way. But she didn't look like herself. The girl in the mirror was someone she didn't know!

She wondered what everyone back home—especially the real Thanatos and Hypnos—would say about her makeover. Her old look was quite fashionable by Underworld standards. This new look would be weird there! That thought made her smile. Well, when at MOA, do as the MOAers do, she thought.

"Thanks," she told Aphrodite politely.

"You're welcome," Aphrodite replied, obviously

proud of her work. With her hands on her hips, she eyed the black chiton Nyx was wearing. "Now that we've redone your makeup, that black outfit has got to go," she said gently but firmly. "As soon as school is out we'll find you something else to wear." She looked around at the other girls. "My wardrobe is mostly pink—not a good color for Nyx. Maybe some of you could let her try on outfits from your closets to find some things she could borrow this week?"

Shouts of "I'll do it!" and "Sure!" went up right away. For the moment these girls seemed to have forgotten to be wary of her.

Nyx smiled around at the volunteers. She appreciated their eagerness to help, though she still wasn't sure what was wrong with black. No matter. She was now determined to change her style this week, just to experience life as a normal MOA goddessgirl.

Aphrodite and Artemis were in the same classes together for both fourth and fifth periods. So when Beauty-ology let out, Nyx accompanied them down the hall to their fifth-period class, Revenge-ology. A lot of heads turned her way as they walked, only now the stares seemed much friendlier than the ones she'd received when she'd arrived yesterday and again this morning. Yes!

By the time the three girls joined other students in the fourth floor dorm after school, Nyx was feeling more comfortable with her new look. She was even looking forward to trying on new (non-black) outfits.

"We can use my room as a dressing room," Aphrodite told everyone. Nodding, the girls scattered to their rooms to riffle through their closets for outfits Nyx could try on.

"While everyone's getting clothes, I'll go make

sure my parakeets have seed and water," Nyx remarked. This wasn't exactly necessary, since she'd fed her birds a few hours ago. Still, she was a teeny bit concerned about Hypnos and Thanatos being alone with Artemis's dogs.

"If my dogs try to jump on you, just tell them to get down," Artemis called after her. "I'll stay here and help Aphrodite get stuff ready. We'll need snacks!"

"Okay. Back in a jiff," Nyx replied. Since Artemis's room was right next door, Nyx was there almost instantly. The dogs did indeed jump up on her first thing, their tails wagging back and forth. "Get down," she told them firmly, and after a few seconds they obeyed and went to lie on the floor.

Standing on tiptoe, Nyx lifted the birdcage down from the shelf above Artemis's spare desk. She cooed to her birds, "Did you miss me?"

But then her eyes went wide in alarm. Because although the cage door was closed tight, there was only *one* bird inside the cage—Hypnos. Her gaze flashed wildly around the room. "Thanatos! Where are you?"

And then her eyes fell on a yellow feather on the floor under the desk. Instantly, she leaped to the conclusion that Thanatos had somehow gotten out of the cage. And worse, that he'd been eaten by one of Artemis's dogs! Her hand flew to her mouth. "Nooooo!" she screamed.

8

Gone

FOOTSTEPS CAME RUNNING. FOUR GODDESSGIRLS burst through the door and peered around Artemis's room, but Nyx's anxious shadowy mist hung in the air, making it difficult to see clearly.

"What's going on?" Aphrodite called out.

"Thanatos—one of my birds is gone!" wailed Nyx. She carefully set the cage back onto its high shelf. She didn't want to drop it and hurt Hypnos!

Excited by all the sudden activity, Artemis's dogs leaped around. "Lie down! Stay!" Artemis ordered. As Persephone helped her round them up, Athena and Aphrodite rushed to Nyx's side.

"Tell us what happened," coaxed Athena.

Nyx managed to calm herself enough to speak, which caused her shadowy mist to slowly disappear. Still, tears were running down her cheeks as she pointed up at the birdcage. "Thanatos got out somehow and I . . . I think one of Artemis's dogs *ate* him!" She scooped up the yellow feather from the floor and held it out for the others to see.

As if aware of being in trouble, Artemis's dogs stopped wagging their tails. They lowered their heads to their paws and whimpered.

A horrified look came over Artemis's face. "What? No!" she exclaimed. She grabbed Suez's big head and pried open his jaws. Then she peered inside as if checking for evidence—like a yellow feather caught in his teeth or something.

Meanwhile Athena carefully lifted down the bird-cage. After setting it on top of the desk, she began checking the bars of the cage. "Look," she said, pushing on one of the bars. "It's not attached to the bottom of the cage. I bet it jiggled loose somehow. Maybe on your trip here."

"That must be how Thanatos got out," said Aphrodite.

"Nope, no feathers," said Artemis after checking Amby's and Nectar's mouths too.

"The window is open," Persephone pointed out. She looked at Nyx. "So maybe Artemis's dogs didn't eat your bird. Maybe it flew away."

All five girls crowded around the window to look

outside. But there was no sign of the green-and-yellow parakeet. Or of any additional feathers on the ground below the window, either. Not that that necessarily proved anything, of course.

"If he did fly outside, would he come back if you called him?" asked Aphrodite.

"Possibly, if I whistle and he's close enough to hear," Nyx said, brightening a little. Leaning her head out the window, she whistled and whistled, making sounds that resembled parakeet chirps. But Thanatos didn't appear.

Aphrodite sighed. "Adonis is not great at coming when he's called, either."

The mention of Adonis only caused another dark mist to briefly swirl around Nyx. What if Thanatos had flown outside to escape being eaten by Artemis's dogs and had somehow met his doom with the cat, instead?

Seeing the mist and guessing what she was thinking, Persephone said quickly, "Adonis has been in Aphrodite's room all day. And her window is closed, so Thanatos couldn't have flown in there."

"Even if Thanatos didn't get eaten, he's still lost . . . or something," Nyx said gloomily as she continued to stare out the window.

Persephone slid an arm around Nyx's shoulders. "Maybe he'll find his way back soon. Stay hopeful."

Nyx nodded. But it was hard to dislodge the feeling of doom that had settled at the bottom of her stomach.

"We could try to look for him," Athena suggested. "Although it might be like looking for a needle in a haystack."

"No telling how long he's been gone," Artemis added. "He could have already escaped before

I brought my dogs upstairs at the start of fourth period. I didn't check the cage, so if he wasn't in there I wouldn't have known."

Nyx's face crumpled and a few tears streamed down her face. She wiped them away, probably smearing Aphrodite's makeup job in the process, she thought. "I hope he'll be okay. I hope he finds food and water."

"How about if I ask Hephaestus to fix the bar on your birdcage to keep your other bird from escaping?" Aphrodite offered. "He's the godboy of metalworking."

Someone handed Nyx some tissues and she managed to dry her tears. "Okay, thanks," she said dully.

The girls sprang into action, eager to help. Athena made sure the window was firmly closed, but stood by it, keeping an eye out for Thanatos's possible

return. Artemis rounded up her dogs. "C'mon, boys. Walkies. Let's get out of everyone's way." Then to the girls, she added, "I'll be on the lookout for the bird. And I'll tell Pheme about Thanatos and have her spread the word for everyone else to do the same."

After she and the dogs left, Nyx opened the cage and coaxed Hypnos onto her finger. Then she carefully transferred him to the top of the desk. Since Artemis had apparently already emptied her trash basket, Persephone turned the woven basket upside down and helped Nyx lower it over the parakeet to create a makeshift cage for the bird beneath the basket on the desktop. Afterward, Aphrodite took the metal cage with the loose bar and went to find Hephaestus.

With Persephone's help, Nyx began looking

around the room for small containers in which to place seed and water for the bird.

"This probably isn't the best time to ask this," Athena said from her guard post at the window, "but I talked to Hera before breakfast this morning about babysitting Hebe tonight. She asked me to ask you if she could borrow your birds." Athena hesitated before adding, "I guess you talked to Dad about it yesterday? Something about their singing possibly helping Hebe sleep better?"

"Yeah. Only that was before Thanatos went missing! Now I'm not . . ." Nyx's voice trailed off. Though reluctant to let Hera borrow her only remaining parakeet, she genuinely wanted to be of help. Making up her mind, she said, "If the cage gets fixed so it's definitely secure, then you can take Hypnos with you when you go to babysit."

"Really? Are you sure?" Athena asked. "With Thanatos gone, Hera and Dad will understand if you've changed your mind."

"Of course they will," Persephone said sympathetically. Having found and filled containers with seed and water, she and Nyx were working to slip them under the basket without letting Hypnos escape.

Nyx thought about what Athena had said. "Do Zeus and Hera have a cat or a dog? Or anything that could endanger a bird?"

"No," Athena assured her. "Just Hebe. And a baby's no danger to anyone, that is, unless they're trying to sleep."

Despite her sadness over Thanatos, Nyx managed a small smile. "Then Hypnos will probably be just as safe at Zeus and Hera's place as here. One thing though. He won't sing if it's dark," she told

Athena. "So Hera will need to leave a light in the room with his cage."

"Not a problem," Athena reminded her. "My dad sleeps with a night-light, remember? He's got a lamp decorated with little winged horses." Suddenly Athena yawned big.

Leaving Hypnos for the moment, Nyx went and sat on the spare bed. She hugged a pillow covered with a dog-bone-patterned pillowcase to her chest. It gave her some small comfort.

"What is it with everyone yawning around here today?" asked Persephone, plopping down on Artemis's bed.

"Sorry," said Athena. "Hardly got any sleep. I had the worst nightmare about a test in Hero-ology class. I'd forgotten all about having to take it and was totally unprepared. In fact, I hadn't even been going to class because I thought it was summer vacation!"

"Just the kind of nightmare the brainiest goddess-girl at MOA *would* have," Persephone said affectionately. "I slept fine."

"Hmm," mused Athena. "But you were at home, not here." Abruptly, she straightened and turned from the window, looking like she was thinking hard. "Aphrodite had nightmares too. Remember how she said she only got half her usual beauty sleep last night?"

Nyx and Persephone both nodded.

Athena went on. "In Hero-ology this morning she told me she'd dreamed she was allergic to makeup. The dream woke her up and she ran to check a mirror to see if she really did have swollen lips and a rash all over her face. She didn't, of course, but then she bumped into something and stubbed her toe."

Persephone grimaced. "Ouch."

"I hope everyone's trouble sleeping doesn't have anything to do with me being here," Nyx said in alarm. She let go of the pillow and got up from the bed. Then she began to pace back and forth on the rug between the two beds. "I'm in charge of night, not dreams. That's the Oneiroi's job. Still, it's possible my powers are having some weird magnifying effect on the dreams around here." She winced at the word "weird."

"Hades told me about the Oneiroi," said Persephone. "Three brothers who live in the Underworld, right?"

Nyx stopped pacing to face the two goddessgirls. "Mm-hm. In Tartarus, near me actually. Morpheus is the most powerful of them, so he oversees the dreams of heroes and kings. He's especially good

at creating mega-realistic images of humans." She paused, trying to catch hold of a thought floating at the far edge of her consciousness. But she couldn't quite bring the thought forward.

Athena's intelligent gray-blue eyes regarded her keenly. "What about his brothers? What kind of dreams do they create?"

Nyx wondered if their questions were just intended to help her get her mind off Thanatos. Talking about something else *was* helping. A little bit, anyway. "Let's see, Phobetor is in charge of nightmares. He can conjure images of huge, scary animals."

"Like the giant scorpion that chased Apollo?" Athena asked.

"Pretty much," said Nyx. "And the third brother, Phantasus, specializes in illusions."

Persephone cocked her head. "Like Aphrodite dreaming she had a makeup allergy?"

"Sure, sounds right," said Nyx. "The images the brothers conjure up are somewhat muted—dreamlike, I guess you'd say. That's because dreams have to pass through the Underworld before reaching anyone on Earth or Mount Olympus."

Athena raised an eyebrow. "So that's why most dreams don't wake you up and you don't even remember them in the morning, I suppose."

"Yeah," said Nyx. She frowned as that thought in her consciousness bobbed closer to the surface of her mind. Before she could reel it in, Aphrodite was back.

"Good as new," she announced, handing the repaired cage to Nyx. "Hephaestus soldered the broken bar back in place. He also checked all the other bars to make sure they were firmly attached."

"That was nice of him," said Nyx. She'd tell him so if she got a chance to meet him.

Quickly, the girls transferred Hypnos from the trash basket to the cage. "I don't suppose you'd still like to try on some chitons?" Aphrodite said. "There are at least a half dozen in my room that various girls brought over."

Nyx shook her head. "I need to get more rest before I head out for the night." She didn't really think she'd be able to sleep. She just needed to be alone with her sorrow over Thanatos for a while. From the look the other three goddessgirls traded, she figured they'd guessed what she'd left unsaid.

"We understand," Aphrodite said gently. "Maybe another time."

"When are you supposed to babysit tonight?" Nyx asked Athena as the girls went to the door.

"At seven," Athena replied. "Want me to come by and get Hypnos after dinner?"

Nyx nodded and the three MOA girls departed, closing the door softly behind them.

Just in case Thanatos was still alive and able to find his way back to her, Nyx reopened the window. Speaking to Hypnos through the bars of his cage, she said, "I bet you miss your buddy. Is that why you've been so quiet?" Hypnos had hardly made a peep since Thanatos's disappearance. Maybe he was comforted by Nyx's voice because now he began to sing. Nyx lay down to rest, and, despite thinking she wouldn't be able to, she soon fell asleep.

She awoke sometime later to a rattling noise. Her eyes flew open and she leaped from her bed. "Thanatos?" she called out. She imagined he'd flown in through the open window and was rattling the bars of his cage, trying to get back inside. But it was Hypnos who was rattling the bars. He was testing each of them with his beak. Probably wanting to get out and find his dear friend, Nyx thought.

"I miss him too," she told Hypnos. New tears began to slip down her cheeks.

With a sigh she brushed them away, and then turned toward the window. She could see from the sundial below that it was nearly time for her to go to work. She'd slept longer than she'd meant to, so there'd be no time to grab dinner in the cafeteria.

But as she went to ready herself, she noticed that a covered dinner tray had been left on Artemis's bed. There was a note on top of it:

DEAR NYX,

DIDN'T WANT TO WAKE YOU, BUT

HERE'S DINNER IN CASE YOU DON'T HAVE TIME TO STOP BY THE CAFETERIA BEFORE YOU LEAVE. I'M REALLY SORRY ABOUT THANATOS AND FOR ANY PART MY DOGS MIGHT HAVE PLAYED IN HIS DISAPPEARANCE. DOGS ARE STAYING WITH APOLLO FOR THE REST OF THE WEEK.

LATER,

ARTEMIS

Nyx's eyes lingered over the words "any part my dogs might have played." Did that mean Artemis wasn't completely sure that one of her dogs hadn't actually eaten Thanatos? They might never know. Anyway, the tray of food was thoughtful.

After eating, Nyx slipped her magical starry cape

into the pocket of her chiton. Then she grabbed her hairbrush. When she looked in the mirror hanging on the closet door, she was startled anew by Aphrodite's makeover handiwork, the mascara smudged by her recent tears.

She shook her head at her reflection. "Time to be me again," she told it as she finished brushing her hair. Before leaving, she set her mostly finished dinner tray on Artemis's desk. She couldn't help casting a hopeful glance toward the open window. Unfortunately, Thanatos wasn't hovering outside it.

"Bye, Hypnos." After blowing him a kiss, she covered the cage. Then she headed for the bathroom to wash off her makeup and reapply it in her usual goth style before racing downstairs and outside.

9

Fitful Night, Thunderous Morning

SOON NYX HAD DONNED HER STARRY CAPE AND was riding high in her purple and gold chariot, bringing rest to the weary as shadows lengthened and night took over the sky. Alone with her thoughts and the stars, she felt the loss of Thanatos keenly. Not even the squeaky little bats that usually gave her such joy could lighten her mood tonight. Despite her enjoyment of the new experiences she'd been having, she couldn't help thinking that coming to Mount Olympus had been a tragic mistake.

When it was finally time for night to end and she was on her way back to MOA, she glimpsed Eos in the distance. To Nyx's surprise, the goddess of the dawn waved her over. Directing Erebus closer, Nyx saw that Eos held a notescroll tied with a multicolored ribbon in all the colors of the dawn. As the two girls neared each other, Eos tossed the notescroll high.

It fell inside the chariot, landing at Nyx's feet. Huh? What could Eos have to say to her? She picked up the notescroll and was about to unroll it when Erebus made a sharp turn to the right to get her chariot back on course. The turn caught Nyx totally off guard, jerking her so hard she almost fell. She

fumbled with the notescroll, accidentally dropping it over the side of the chariot.

"Oh no!" she cried out. Though she scanned for it from above, she couldn't see it on the forested ground below. She was dying to know what Eos could've written. They'd never even traded greetings before!

Even if she'd had the energy to go looking for the scroll, which she didn't, she would never find it in the trees. Night was over. Already the yellows, oranges, and pinks of dawn were taking over the sky and Eos was far away, with no clue her message had not been read. Leaving the scroll to lie wherever it had fallen, Nyx made for the Academy. Her chariot landed beside the stables and she hopped down from it. After a kiss to Erebus's nose and a fond stroke along his mane, she snapped him and the chariot away.

With Pheme spreading the word, it seemed likely to Nyx that most MOA students would have heard about her parakeet's disappearance by now. Not wanting to face their questions about what happened *or* their pity, she lingered near the stables to pet Pegasus in his stall.

Only when she heard the herald *ping* his lyrebell and announce the start of first-period classes did Nyx hurry inside and up to Artemis's room. She was surprised not to hear the dogs at the door when she twisted the knob, but then she remembered the note Artemis had left. It was probably best that the dogs were with Apollo. Still, Nyx kind of missed their enthusiastic greetings. With the dogs *and* her birds gone, the room was deathly quiet. Ordinarily, anything that could be described as *deathly*, was A-OK with her. But not this time!

After changing into her nightgown and making sure the window was still open for Thanatos's possible return, Nyx climbed into bed as the sun rose higher. With Thanatos missing and Hypnos with Zeus, Hera, and baby Hebe, there was no birdsong to lull her to sleep. Even with the covers over her head to block the daylight, she tossed and turned. Finally she did drop off, only to sleep fitfully. Nightmares disturbed her, including one in which she came upon a group of giant snarling sharp-toothed monsters that were munching away on bird feathers. (No need to wonder what had inspired *that* nightmare!)

She had only just dropped down to a deeper level of sleep when she was startled awake by someone pounding on her door. "It's me—Athena!" a frantic voice called out. "I need to talk to you!"

Nyx sat up in bed and rubbed her eyes. "Come

in," she said sleepily. Judging from the light outside, it couldn't be later than ten o'clock. What was so urgent that Athena felt the need to wake her, unless . . . "Is Hypnos okay?" Nyx asked anxiously as the goddessgirl burst into the room.

"Fine," Athena said quickly. "For now."

Huh? What was that supposed to mean? Before Nyx could ask, Athena went on. "I came to warn you that Dad's on the rampage."

Nyx stared at her in confusion. "I don't understand. Oh, so Hypnos's singing didn't help Hebe sleep better after all?" If the baby had slept worse than usual last night, that would explain Zeus's anger.

But Athena shook her head. "Quite the opposite. It did help. She slept great."

Nyx quirked an eyebrow. "Then . . . ?"

Athena went to the window, gazing down at the courtyard as if expecting something to appear as she continued explaining. "Hypnos's singing also made Zeus and Hera sleep well. *Too* well. When some sailors devoted to Zeus tried to alert him to come to their aid because their ship was in danger of sinking, he failed to hear their summons."

"Uh-oh," said Nyx. Looking out for mortals was an important part of Zeus's job as King of the Gods.

"Yeah," said Athena, turning away from the window to pace and wring her hands. "Those sailors nearly drowned! They depend on Dad, and in their eyes he let them down. Dad blames you. He thinks that you and your bird intentionally made him oversleep."

"What? No!" Nyx's eyes went wide. How could Zeus think that? But this was serious! If mortals came

to doubt Zeus's ability to rule well, which included helping them out in emergencies, they might just give their support to some other ruler! "Where's Hypnos?" she asked, suddenly afraid for her pet.

Before Athena could answer, a bolt of lightning suddenly lit up the sky outside, which had turned an angry gray. A loud peal of thunder followed almost instantly. Both girls jumped at the sound and then rushed to look out the window. Zeus was running around in the courtyard now, tossing thunderbolts into the air right and left as a blue-and-white parakeet dodged them.

"I'll fricassee you, you dumb bird, you!" he boomed. "Come back here!"

Squawk! Squawk! Hypnos sounded scared.

"Oh no!" cried Nyx. "Zeus is going to hurt him if this keeps up!" A black mist began to swirl around

her as her fear grew, and the roiling wind pulled curls of it outside.

Hypnos must have seen the mist and realized what it meant because he made a beeline for the window and the safety she could provide. He flew inside just as another of Zeus's thunderbolts struck the outside wall of the Academy right beside the window. BOOM! Trembling with fear, Hypnos landed on Nyx's shoulder and sidestepped till he was right up against her neck and partly hidden under her thick hair.

Athena leaned out the window. "Dad! Stop!" she called out. "It was not a plot that you overslept last night, I promise!"

Zeus had drawn his arm back, about to launch another thunderbolt, but now he let his arm drop to his side. "Theenie?" He peered up at her.

Gathering her courage, Nyx fanned away the black

mist and poked her head forward so she'd be spotted.

"You!" Zeus shouted up at her, now that he could clearly see her standing next to Athena. "Hand over that bird! Do you realize the trouble and *harm* he almost caused?"

"It wasn't on purpose," Nyx dared to say. "And I *won't* hand him over!" she added defiantly.

From beside her, Athena gasped. One did not disobey the King of the Gods. *Ever.* Expecting him to raise his arm with the thunderbolt again and incinerate her, Nyx cringed. Then to her surprise, Zeus backed down.

"Fine," he growled. "Keep him, then. But you'll both have to go. *Immediately.*"

"But, Dad," Athena called down. "That's not fair. She was invited to stay for a week, and it's only been two d—"

At the same time Nyx stammered, "B-but what about my other bird? I need to be here in case Thanatos comes—"

"Silence!" thundered Zeus. He glowered at Nyx so darkly that this time she obeyed. No way did she want to anger Zeus further and make him change his mind about sparing Hypnos's life.

"Go now, and make it snappy," Zeus growled up at her. "I don't want to find you here when I get back from trying to save my reputation. Thanks to your dumb bird, everything is a mess!"

Turning abruptly, he strode off toward the stables. Probably planning to fly down to Earth on Pegasus to meet with those sailors and other mortals, Nyx guessed. To make the case that he could still be depended on to protect them in times of need.

"I'm so sorry," Athena apologized after Zeus had

left. “This wasn’t your fault, you know. Dad might be in a more reasonable state of mind after he fixes things up with the sailors. If you want, I can talk to him after he’s back and—”

“Thanks,” said Nyx, closing the window. “But I’d better do as he said and go.”

Sounding resigned, Athena said, “Okay. Yeah.”

“Could you get Hypnos’s cage from Hera while I get ready?” Nyx asked her.

“Of course,” said Athena. She headed for the door, looking almost as miserable as Nyx felt.

Hypnos perched on the shelf where his cage had sat yesterday, while Nyx changed from her nightgown into a chiton. She gathered her belongings, and then she was ready to go. As she sat on the edge of Artemis’s spare bed to wait for Athena’s return, she held out her upturned palm. Her bird flew down to

sit upon it. "This visit didn't exactly turn out the way we hoped, did it?" she said to Hypnos sadly. Tears sprang into her eyes, but she wiped them away.

Moments later, Athena was back with the bird-cage. Hera had come with her. The statuesque goddess, whose thick blond hair was piled high on her head, was cradling Hebe in her arms. The baby was in a good mood—all smiley and giggly.

"I'm sorry about this," Hera said as Nyx slid open the cage gate and gently deposited Hypnos inside. "You've been a big help. Last night Hebe slept for the longest time in forever." She smiled at Nyx. "And so did I. It was *heaven*." She hesitated, and then in a near echo of Athena's earlier words, she said, "Wait a while. When Zeus returns I'll speak to him on your behalf. Sometimes I can get him to see reason."

Nyx waved away her offer. "Thanks, but I think

it's best if I go." Though she didn't say so, staying would be humiliating. The entire school must've seen Zeus's thunderworks display and heard what he'd said to her. Even when he wasn't angry, he wasn't exactly quiet!

Tears pricked her eyes again as she stood. The lack of sleep probably wasn't helping her mood, either. Thing was, she felt like she'd been starting to convince everyone here that she wasn't so bad and that night had value, but now she wouldn't have a chance to finish the job. She'd been foolish to think that she could ever fit in and become just one of the girls—even for a week.

Hera passed Hebe to Athena so she could give Nyx a fond farewell hug. "Please know that I wish you well."

"Thank you," Nyx said around the lump in her

throat. She hoped Athena appreciated what a nice stepmother she had.

After Hera and Hebe left, Nyx took the birdcage with Hypnos inside and Athena lifted her black travel bag. The girls started downstairs. They'd just reached the front doors when the lyrebell *ping*ed to indicate the start of third period. "I wish I could stay to see you off, but I've got a test in Science-ology this period," Athena said hurriedly.

"It's okay. I can manage," said Nyx, realizing that Athena must've skipped part of second period to be with her.

"If Thanatos shows up, I'll send you a message. Promise," said Athena. After a quick, heartfelt hug, she handed over Nyx's bag and raced off to class.

With her bag in one hand and Hypnos's cage in the other, Nyx pushed through the doors and started

outside. She wished she had time to say good-bye to some of the other girls, especially Artemis. But then that very goddessgirl appeared before her.

Artemis eyed her luggage. "I heard and saw everything from the Hero-ology class windows. I should be in Beast-ology right now, but I got permission from Professor Ladon to come see you off."

Nyx sent her a sad smile before the two girls headed down the granite stairs. The moment she reached the MOA courtyard, Nyx snapped her fingers, bringing forth Erebus and the chariot in a swirl of silver glitter. After tossing her sparkly black bag into the chariot, she set the birdcage alongside it.

When she turned around, Artemis handed her a small bag she'd been carrying. "Snacks," she announced. "I stopped by the cafeteria and got them for your trip back to the Underworld."

"Thanks! You're so sweet," Nyx told her. Of all the students at MOA, Artemis was her favorite. Of course, Artemis was goddess of the moon in addition to the hunt. Maybe that shared connection to the night sky contributed to her feeling of friendship for the girl. She sensed that Artemis liked her a lot too. "I'll—I'll miss you," Nyx added. She gave Artemis a hug.

"Safe trip home," Artemis bade her as Nyx climbed aboard. "I wish things had gone better, but it wasn't your fault."

It wasn't your fault. Athena had used practically the same words when she'd apologized for Zeus banishing Nyx. But Nyx *did* blame herself. She should have known better than to think she could change minds or influence anyone's thinking about her and her precious night. Her coming to MOA had done more damage than good.

Salvaging what was left of her pride, however, she plastered a big smile on her face. "Bye! Let me know if Thanatos turns up!" she called to Artemis. Then she urged her horse "onward and upward."

10

Things Get Worse

AS EREBUS SAILED THE CHARIOT IN THE direction of the Underworld, Nyx thought with dread about what she would say to the real Hypnos and Thanatos upon her return. Even though the brothers were way older than she was, they were the closest thing to friends that she had. They knew she was supposed to be staying at MOA for a week. And they'd been super excited for her when she'd

showed them her invitation and the essay Athena and Artemis had sent along with it.

Word of her banishment would spread quickly, even to the Underworld. It didn't matter that Pheme, the prime source of gossip and rumor at MOA and on Earth, wasn't allowed down there. When some newly deceased mortal crossed over the River Styx, the news would leak out. Nyx sighed, not looking forward to witnessing the looks of disappointment on those elderly brothers' faces.

When Erebus was halfway to the spot where he would begin his descent to the Underworld, it began to sprinkle lightly. Soon the sprinkles became full-fledged raindrops, and as the drops fell faster and harder, they turned into a downpour. Spying a cave in the trees below, Nyx guided Erebus toward it, thinking she could rest there till the rain slowed

(or better, *stopped*) before continuing on. With luck she'd still make it back home before she had to leave again to perform her nightly job.

By the time she landed, Nyx was drenched to the bone. She left her chariot outside the cave and tied her horse to a nearby tree. She could have snapped him and the chariot away, but Erebus was unusual in that he actually liked rain showers, so she'd let him enjoy this one till she was ready to leave again.

Quickly, she emptied her chariot, bringing everything inside: Hypnos in his cage, her sparkly black bag, and the snacks Artemis had given her. Unlike the horse, her bird did not like rain. Once he was inside the cave, Hypnos gave his feathers a good shake to dry them. Then, because it was dark in there, he tucked his head to his breast and fell asleep.

Nyx gathered some dry boughs she'd found

under an overhang outside the cave and brought them inside to sit on. As she was spreading them on the floor, she found a scroll buried among them. She examined it. It was damp and crushed, but she immediately recognized it as the one Eos had tossed to her yesterday morning. Her chariot must've been flying over these very woods when she'd fumbled and dropped the notescroll, she realized. So this was where it had fallen!

As soon as she was settled upon the boughs, she took her blue-black cape from her bag and pulled it around herself for warmth. In the darkness, its stars winked on and off. Unless she waved it outward to expand it, her cape's magic would remain safely contained by the cave. She didn't need to worry about it causing a premature night to fall upon the rest of the world!

At last she turned her attention to Eos's notescroll

again. Though exhausted from too little sleep and too much emotion, she was curious about its contents. After slipping off the scroll's multicolored ribbon, she unrolled it.

Though it was dark inside the cave, her cape gave off just enough starlight to read by. As Nyx read, her eyes widened with alarm:

DEAR NYX,

I SPOTTED THE ONEIROI FLITTING AROUND OUTSIDE MOA AS I ROSE IN THE SKY THIS MORNING.

THOUGHT YOU'D WANT TO KNOW.

HOW THEY ESCAPED THE UNDERWORLD IS A MYSTERY.

MAYBE YOU SHOULD ALERT HADES?

ALL BEST,

EOS, GODDESS OF THE DAWN

P.S. NICE TO MEET YOU!

The Oneiroi escaped!? Nyx pursed her lips as she stared at Eos's notescroll. This was not good! But how had they . . . ? Suddenly the puzzle pieces fell into place.

"Oh no!" she moaned, flopping backward to lie on the boughs. Two days ago, when Nyx had first arrived at MOA . . . Those shadows Artemis had seen fly out of Nyx's bag in the office must've been the three Oneiroi! Nyx had been sure Artemis had just imagined them. She'd even told Artemis so.

And later, she herself had glimpsed a shadowy form zooming out of Zeus's office window as he slept. She'd chalked the vision up to imagination contagion, or maybe evidence of some weird atmospheric disturbance that was a result of her presence at MOA. But now she decided it had in fact been that tricky trio. They must have hitched a ride in her black bag when she'd left the Underworld!

Suddenly the weird dreams and nightmares various students at the Academy had been having the last two nights all made sense. Why hadn't she made the connection between those dreams and the Oneiroi before? She'd had a lot on her mind, that's why! A missing bird and her mission to convince everyone at MOA how great the night was, for example.

As long as dreams had to travel all the way up from the Underworld, their power was mild. But if the Oneiroi had really gotten loose within the Academy, their very nearness to students and staff would increase the power and impact of the dreams they created tenfold or more. She jumped up. She

had to go back to MOA and fix things! And take the Oneiroi back to the Underworld, where those rascals belonged!

She hurried to the cave's entrance. Outside it was still raining hard. Great sheets of water washed down from the sky. She would have to wait. Besides, she was *sooo* tired, she thought as she stuffed the notescroll in the pocket of her damp chiton. She tried to keep her eyes open as she lay back on the dry boughs, but her eyelids were much too heavy. Before she knew it, she'd drifted into an uneasy sleep.

Sometime later, Nyx awoke suddenly to hear strange noises outside the cave. Not rain. That seemed to have stopped. No, she heard slithering sounds. And frightened whinnies. Erebus! With her cape still wrapped around her, she crept toward the cave's opening. When she saw what was outside, she gasped. A gigantic monster was menacing her horse! Though it was a beautiful woman on top, it was a fierce-looking snake down below.

Of all the caves Nyx could have chosen, she'd somehow chosen this monster's! She twisted her hands together. Oh, why hadn't she snapped Erebus safely off in a silver burst when she'd first landed? She would do it now, but she had to be looking directly into his eyes to make the magic work. And the monster was blocking the way.

Scared out of her wits, Nyx walked backward toward the boughs. She slipped off her cape, down-sized it, and shoved it into her bag so that its starry light wouldn't shine out and pinpoint her location within the cave. Batting away the black mist of anx-iety swirling around her, she gathered her courage. "Leave my horse alone!" she shouted.

The monster's long black hair whirled around its massive shoulders as it whipped its head in the direction of Nyx's voice. "Who's been sleeping in Echidna's cave? Echidna, mother of monsters, does not tolerate interlopers."

Huh? Nyx shuddered to think about the idea of *baby* monsters! She had to get her horse, bird, and self out of here before any of those showed up. At that very moment Erebus managed to pull free from both the tree *and* the chariot. But before she could catch his eye and *snap* him off to safety, he galloped away.

The monster's black eyes flashed with anger and its speckled snake-body writhed. "That horse was going to be Echidna's supper!" it screeched. "Echidna will find you. And then she will make a meal out of you instead!"

It was weird the way this monster spoke in third person, as if it were royalty, which Nyx seriously doubted. She backed away quickly as the monster slithered closer and peered into the entrance. Its eyes darted here and there, trying to see deeper into the dark cave through the black mist of anxiety that surrounded Nyx anew.

There was no way out now. And even if Nyx could manage to grab Hypnos's cage and flee, what would she do then? Erebus had bolted, and she doubted she could outrun an enormous half serpent.

"Come out, come out, whoever you are," Echidna singsonged.

Since the serpent-woman couldn't seem to spot her in the dim cave, Nyx dared to speak again. "Eating me would not be a good idea! I'm the goddess of the night, and it's getting late. Almost time for me to begin to darken the sky. If you don't let me go after my horse, there will be no night, um, to*night*. You'll have to start calling it to*light* from now on."

After feeling around for Hypnos's cage, Nyx hugged it to her and scampered even deeper into the cave.

"Ha!" *Thump* went the monster's serpent tail. "All the better! If the sun always shines outside Echidna's lair, it will be easier to see any prey that ventures by."

Nyx tried a different tack. "Still, you risk angering both immortals and mortals if you keep me here."

Echidna laughed. "Perhaps you overestimate your importance, goddess of the night. Many immortals and mortals fear darkness. They will not miss you. Echidna might even become a hero for dispensing with you."

Could this monster mommy be right? Would it become the next unsung hero for doing away with her? Just then

Nyx heard the trot of hooves outside the cave.

Then, slithering sounds, and, "Gotcha!"

Had Erebus returned only to be eaten? *Nooo!* Still holding the birdcage, Nyx leaped toward the cave entrance, where she saw . . . tusks. Echidna had captured a wild boar! Nyx closed her eyes and covered her ears as best she could so as not to hear the disgusting, crunching sounds the monster made as it devoured its prey.

When Nyx finally worked up the courage to open her eyes and uncover her ears, she heard Echidna give a satisfied burp. "That was tasty," said the monster, slithering its way back into the cave. "Filling, too. So you're safe for now, goddess of the night. In fact, Echidna may not eat you at all if trapping you here really does bring more daylight, and therefore more food, to Echidna's door."

Nyx skittered farther back into the darkness, stopping at a distant point where she could still keep an eye on the monster. Meanwhile, Echidna coiled up snakelike, blocking the cave's opening and only exit. The monster's head dropped down to rest on the topmost coil. "Don't even *think* about trying to escape," it warned Nyx. "Echidna sleeps with one eye open. If you try to sneak past, you'll be toast in two shakes of my tail."

Nyx swallowed hard. Having seen how fast this monster had nabbed that boar, she could believe it. With her arms wrapped around Hypnos's cage, she sank lower till she was sitting on the ground. After Zeus had ordered her to leave the Academy, she'd thought that things couldn't get any worse. Turned out she'd been wrong.

Her visit had set off a string of disasters. Thanatos

and Erebus were gone, she'd gotten Zeus in trouble with mortals, and she'd accidentally unleashed the Oneiroi on MOA! To top it all off, she was now trapped in this cave with Echidna. Filled with despair, she curled herself around Hypnos and his cage to sleeplessly await the long night . . . uh . . . *day* ahead.

11

Day After Day

Meanwhile, back at MOA . . .

IT WASN'T UNTIL AFTER DINNER THAT THE students and staff at Mount Olympus Academy began to notice that something strange was going on. Namely, that the color of the sky had not changed. It remained just as bright now as it had been at noon.

As the evening hours ticked by, the goddess-girls grew increasingly worried that something had

happened to Nyx. And by the time they walked back from the sports fields after their evening Cheer practice, they could all see that Helios the sun god's chariot was now so low in the sky that it would soon disappear below the horizon. Yet the sky had not changed color or darkened. Not even one tiny bit.

"What do you think is going on?" Artemis said to her three BFFs, grimly clutching her blue-and-gold pom-poms to her chest as they walked along.

"Maybe Hades and I should visit the Underworld," Persephone suggested. "To check to see if Nyx made it there okay."

"Good idea," said Aphrodite. "And I'll find Pheme. She might know if Nyx said anything to anyone about planning to stop somewhere along the way home."

Athena looked at Artemis. "Zeus must have

noticed that the sky is still as blue as morning, too. But in case he hasn't, we should go talk to him."

Artemis nodded. Though Athena hadn't said so, it was likely they were both thinking the same thing. That tired and grumpy as Zeus had been lately, it really was possible he hadn't noticed the sky was still light.

At the entrance to the Academy the goddessgirls separated to pursue the various tasks they'd set for themselves. The minute Artemis and Athena stepped inside the school, they met Hera. She was carrying a giggling and well-rested (for once!) Hebe in her arms. "Zeus still hasn't returned from seeing those sailors," she said when Athena asked about him.

Most students had heard Zeus yelling at Nyx about the sailors' being unable to rouse him when their ship had been about to sink. He must still be trying to fix the trouble he blamed Hypnos for, Artemis thought.

After the two goddessgirls explained what they'd wanted to see Zeus about, Hera looked at the sky in surprise. "I must admit I've been so wrapped up in Hebe, I hadn't even realized that it should be getting dark by now." Her forehead wrinkled in thought. "Do you think Nyx was so upset at having to leave MOA that it caused her to neglect her duties? Temporarily, anyway?"

"Never," Artemis said loyally. In truth, though, that thought *had* occurred to her. Only she'd dismissed it because she didn't want to believe that Nyx would let her feelings keep her from doing her very important job.

"I'm not sure," Athena hedged, toying with the pom-poms she still held.

Hera smiled down at Hebe, who was gurgling cutely now. Then, tearing her eyes away from the baby, she said to the girls, "I suggest waiting till Zeus is back before taking action. After all, what's the harm in missing one night? Agreed?" Somewhat reluctantly, Athena and Artemis nodded.

Later that night . . . er, *long day* . . . the two goddessgirls met Aphrodite in her room. "I talked to Pheme," Aphrodite informed them as she petted Adonis. The kitten had curled up in her lap the minute she'd sat down on her bed and was now purring contentedly.

"Yeah?" prompted Artemis as she and Athena got comfortable across the room on the spare bed.

"Pheme had already grilled a bunch of people at MOA for information about Nyx," said Aphrodite. "Seems that except for you two and Hera, Nyx didn't directly tell anyone else she was leaving, much less whether she had plans to go anywhere besides the Underworld."

"It's not like her leaving was some big secret, though," Athena said wryly. "Probably everyone heard my dad order her to go. He wasn't exactly subtle."

Artemis wandered over to the window and glanced down at the sundial. It wasn't working, however. Despite the blue sky, the sun had gone below the horizon and could cast no shadow. Still, Artemis guessed that it had to be at least eleven p.m.!

Just as she was wondering when Persephone would be back from the Underworld, a quick knock sounded at the door and Persephone came bursting in. "Hades and I asked around about Nyx," she informed the other three girls. "Nobody has seen her since she left Tartarus last Sunday to come here."

"You didn't tell anyone that Zeus kicked Nyx out, did you?" Artemis asked worriedly. "That would be so embarrassing for her, and—"

With a shake of her head, Persephone interrupted. "No, we didn't tell, but you know how it is. Word will get around soon enough." She paused. "Anyway, here's what's really weird. The Oneiroi are missing from the Underworld!"

"Ye gods! Those dreammaker guys, you mean? That doesn't sound good," said Aphrodite, as Persephone plopped onto the bed beside her.

Artemis frowned as she left the window and came to sit next to Athena. "Do you think it's a coincidence that they're missing too? Could they have kidnapped Nyx?"

"Let's hope not!" Athena exclaimed. Then she sighed. "One more thing for Dad to sort out when he

gets back from talking to the sailors." To Aphrodite and Persephone she added, "Hera advised us to wait until he's back before we do anything more regarding Nyx."

"I wish there was something we could do while waiting," said Artemis.

"Yeah, waiting is hard," Persephone agreed. "But Thanatos and Hypnos—not the birds, the men, I mean—promised to send a message here to let us know when Nyx or the Oneiroi show up."

"Maybe Nyx is just too upset over everything to do her job," Aphrodite added as Adonis stood up in her lap. He stretched, and then hopped over to Persephone's lap.

"You think she could be holed up somewhere between here and the Underworld, nursing hurt feelings?" asked Athena.

“Doesn’t sound like her to me,” said Artemis.

“I bet she’ll be back on the job tomorrow!” Persephone said in a bright voice. To Artemis’s ear, it sounded just a little bit too cheery to reflect her friend’s true feelings.

Aphrodite yawned. “I think it’s time for bed even if it *is* still light out.”

Taking their cue, Artemis and Athena rose from Aphrodite’s spare bed, which was where Persephone would sleep since she was staying over instead of going home.

“Night . . . uh . . . bye, then,” Artemis said.

“See you tomor . . . um . . . at breakfast,” added Athena. Without night to mark the passage of time, the usual expressions just didn’t work!

The next morning, lots of students were late to breakfast. So was the cafeteria staff. And everyone

was grumpy. They'd all found it hard to sleep without darkness. How did Nyx do it? Artemis wondered as she set down her tray of burnt hambrosia and runny eggs and sat next to Aphrodite at the four BFFs' usual table. But then, Nyx was used to a nocturnal existence. Where was that girl, anyway? Artemis thought irritably. As far as she knew, there'd been no messages from the Underworld to say that she'd safely arrived there.

Persephone and Athena were engaged in conversation on the other side of the table and barely seemed to notice Artemis. Aphrodite did, however. "Move your tray," she said crabbily. "It's touching mine."

Artemis felt her temper flare. "Well, *excuuuse* me, Miss Priss." Nevertheless, she moved her tray. But only a fraction of an inch. As Aphrodite stabbed a

fork in her eggs, she glared at her. Artemis noticed that she wasn't wearing makeup for once. And her golden hair was tangled and standing up at the back of her head, as if she'd forgotten to brush it. "Looks like somebody could have used *a lot more* beauty sleep last night, I mean . . . last whatever," Artemis added snarkily.

To her surprise, Aphrodite practically crumbled. She was blinking back tears as she exclaimed, "I barely slept! And every time I did manage to slip off for a few minutes, I was plagued by pesky dreams and nightmares."

"Me too," admitted Artemis, instantly regretting her grumpiness. She had a strong feeling that there was something going on here that she ought to be able to figure out. She shook her head, hoping to clear it, but she was so tired from lack of sleep that her brain just wasn't functioning well.

"I had one dream about an archery competition," she told Aphrodite at last. "The crowd was booing me because my silver arrows kept missing their target over and over and over. Argh!" Missing the target was something that almost never happened to her in real life, thank godness. Before she could ask what Aphrodite's dreams and nightmares had been about, Pheme flitted toward them. Her small iridescent orange wings fluttered at her back, and her sandals barely touched the floor.

"Guess what I just overheard at one of the godboy tables!" she said. Her brown eyes shone with excitement as little cloud letters puffed from her mouth. Persephone's and Athena's attention was caught too, and all four girls focused on the goddess of gossip. Without waiting for guesses, Pheme went on. "Ares had a dream that Gaia turned him into a girl!"

Gaia was the earth goddess, sculpted from mud and rock. She was also the parent of the creature named Typhon—the monster who had menaced Earth and Mount Olympus with his mighty winds not long ago.

Aphrodite giggled the loudest of all four BFFs, her mood improving instantly. Ares, the godboy of war, was her crush, and she adored hearing stories about him.

The idea of becoming a girl would terrify that competitive and athletic godboy, thought Artemis, never mind that many girls were competitive and athletic too. (Take *her*, for example!)

"That's not all," said Pheme, grinning. She loved imparting her tidbits of gossip, especially since doing so made her the center of attention. "Poseidon dreamed that a Geryon sneaked into the boys' bathroom and stole all his tubby toys, including his favorite yellow rubber ducky."

The girls all laughed again. "Hey!" Poseidon yelled indignantly. He was only a table away and was looking up at the words floating above Pheme's head. Reaching upward, Pheme good-naturedly waved them away. It was no secret that the godboy of the sea played with tubby toys, but he was touchy that others found it so amusing.

"I actually had a *good* dream!" Persephone told her friends after Pheme had flitted away to share her gossip with other tables. "I dreamed that my room at home had become a tropical paradise and that everything in it was made of plants, including the seaweed bed I was sleeping in."

That was just the kind of dream that the goddess-

girl of spring and growing things *would* like, Artemis thought fondly.

Just then an argument broke out at a table in the far corner of the cafeteria. "Dude! I did *not* come into your room last night and shoot you with a love arrow to make you fall in love with your pillow! You were dreaming!" A godboy named Eros shouted this at Apollo, who was sitting across from him.

Artemis's jaw dropped, unable to believe her ears.

"You're lying!" Apollo shouted back. "It was real!" He was holding a puffy pillow to his chest. Looking down at it, he said, "Forgive me, dear Puffy. But ours is a love that cannot be!" With that he wrenched the pillow from his arms and heaved it at Eros's head.

Eros put up his arms to block the hit, and the pillow plopped onto his plate.

"Hey!" shouted Apollo in dismay. "You got egg on Puffy!"

Someone must have alerted Mr. Cyclops, MOA's giant one-eyed Hero-ology teacher, that a fight was brewing, because he strode into the cafeteria just then. Looking sternly at Eros and Apollo, he said, "Now I know none of us got much shut-eye last night, but that's no excuse for fighting."

"Shouldn't that be shut-*eyes* for those of us with two of them?" joked Ares.

"Technically, I suppose that's true," said Mr. Cyclops. To his credit, he sounded amused. But then he grew stern again. Pointing to his one eye, and then to the room at large, he said, "There will be no more fighting. I've got my eye on you!"

His threat was effective, and the grumping

quieted down as everyone finished eating. "Do you know if Zeus is back now?" Artemis asked Athena as the four BFFs went to the tray return before exiting the cafeteria. They needed to talk to him and the sooner that better!

Athena shook her head. "Not yet. I saw Hera before breakfast. She sent him a message to let him know what's going on." She paused, yawning. It was catching, and others began to yawn too.

"He must know something's up," Athena went on. "It will have stayed light everywhere in Greece, not just here at MOA."

"Yeah, I bet you're right. Even if he managed to smooth things over with those sailors, he's probably been delayed by other mortals on Earth," Artemis guessed. "They'll be bending his ear with complaints if they got as little rest as everyone here."

The rest of the girls nodded. Then they all yawned again as one.

Over the course of the day everyone, including the teachers, was short-tempered and forgetful due to lack of sleep. Several students fell asleep in class or were simply fuzzy in their thinking when asked to do classroom activities that normally would've given them no trouble.

For instance, when Coach Triathlon asked Artemis to show another student the best way to nock an arrow, she placed the arrow in her bow backward so that its feathered end pointed toward the practice target. To deflect attention from her mistake, she said, "Oops! Sorry. That was just a little nock-nock joke!" Then she reversed her arrow in the proper direction.

And in Beauty-ology Aphrodite had accidentally used a different color shadow on each eyelid. Of course, some mortal girls heard about this and began copying the idea right away, thinking it a new fashion trend.

Finally, just after dinner, the girls saw Zeus fly in on Pegasus. They were out on the sports field at the time, finishing a lackluster Cheer practice. They were all so tired that their leaps were mere hops and their cheers sounded positively funereal. Anxious to talk to Zeus about Nyx, the four friends raced back to the Academy as fast as their weary legs could take them.

When they entered the office, all nine of Ms. Hydra's heads were down on the desk, snoozing. Deciding not to wake her, the girls tiptoed past. They could hear Hebe squalling and Hera and Zeus bickering in Zeus's office.

"Well, if you hadn't lost your temper and thrown thunderbolts at that poor girl's pet bird when she'd only been trying to help us—and then ordered her to leave—maybe this wouldn't have happened!" they heard Hera exclaim.

"What choice did I have?" Zeus countered angrily. "She endangered those sailors and made me appear irresponsible! If mortals can't depend on me—on *all* of us gods—to help in times of need, how long do you think it will be before they stop listening to us and obeying our laws?"

The goddessgirls looked at one another. They were alarmed at the quarreling going on *and* at what Zeus had said. Then, in a softer voice, Zeus added, "So, do you think she's neglecting her duties to spite us?"

Huh? Artemis inhaled sharply. How could Zeus

even *think* that about Nyx? In the short time the girl had been at MOA, Artemis had never seen her be unkind. She'd grown quite fond of Nyx and couldn't believe the girl would want to spite any of them.

"No," Artemis was glad to hear Hera say. "And that worries me even more. At first I thought she might be nursing her wounds. But it's been so long now, I'm beginning to fear that she's in some kind of trouble."

Athena chose that moment to knock on the door. After the girls entered, they used their best babysitting skills (learned in a class taught by Pallas, a mortal friend of Athena's who lived down on Earth) to keep Hebe entertained. That way they could talk to Zeus and Hera about Nyx without interference. As Athena sat in a chair and bounced her baby sister up and down on her knees, Persephone told Zeus and

Hera about her trip to the Underworld with Hades and how Nyx had never shown up there.

Artemis sat on the floor next to Athena and began to play peekaboo with Hebe. The baby giggled in delight each time Artemis covered and uncovered her face.

"And she didn't tell anyone here at MOA about plans to go anywhere except back home to Tartarus," Aphrodite reported.

Zeus frowned. "So we have no leads at all to where she might be."

Artemis stopped the game with Hebe to look up at Zeus. "Maybe teachers and students should form a search party?" In her opinion, they'd already wasted valuable time when they should have been out looking for Nyx!

Zeus's brow furrowed as he considered this idea,

but then he shook his head. "The world is a big place. Nyx could be anywhere. Let's just hang tight and wait for news."

Artemis groaned inwardly in frustration. Still, she could see the wisdom of what Zeus had suggested.

When Persephone brought up the subject of the missing Oneiroi, Artemis suddenly sat up straighter. Despite her tiredness, her brain clicked into gear at last. "I think they're here at MOA!" she exclaimed. "I'm pretty sure I saw them in the office the day Nyx arrived. I saw these shadows whoosh out of her bag and through the office door into the hall!"

Athena put the game of patty-cake she'd begun playing with Hebe on temporary hold. "I remember!" she said in surprise. "Only Nyx said she was sure it wasn't anything. And since I didn't see them myself, I believed her."

She and Artemis exchanged a look. "I believed her too," Artemis admitted. "I was convinced I'd been imagining things."

Zeus's brow furrowed even deeper. "Rounding up those troublemaking rascals won't be easy," he said. "I'll need Hades' help." Then he was out the door.

Soon afterward the girls left too. Artemis felt sick to her stomach. She thought about all the vivid dreams and nightmares everyone at MOA had been having lately. The Oneiroi were the cause. They *had* to be! And Nyx had brought them here. On purpose? Had she planned all along to make trouble? Could Zeus be right that she wanted to spite them? And to think that Artemis and Athena had honored her as an unsung hero! And more than that, Artemis had begun to see her as a true friend!

After another fitful *un*night, Artemis was out walking her dogs before classes began when her hounds began to bark excitedly and pull her toward the stables. Her heart beat fast when she saw Erebus standing outside Pegasus's stall, nuzzling the winged horse's nose. "Nyx?" Artemis called out as her dogs sniffed around the magical horse.

But the goddess didn't answer. "Nyx? Are you here?" Artemis called out again, louder this time. She looked around for Nyx's chariot, but the horse seemed to be on its own. Seeing him here only confused her further. Nyx usually snapped her fingers to make her horse disappear when she wasn't riding it. So what was it doing here, without the chariot? Was she really in some kind of trouble after all?

"So where's Nyx, huh, Erebus?" Artemis asked, giving his muzzle a pat. "Can you take me to her?"

Artemis planned to ask the girl some hard questions if she found her. Like if Nyx had lied about bringing the Oneiroi to MOA!

Unfortunately, despite being magic, Erebus couldn't understand her. Watching her dogs sniff around the magical horse, Artemis suddenly got another idea. Maybe her dogs could find Nyx! After all, they had great noses, especially Suez, her bloodhound. Since the comforter on Nyx's bed hadn't yet been washed, the dogs could get her scent from that. Hopefully it would still be fresh enough to help them track Nyx.

Quickly, Artemis led Nyx's magical horse into the stall next to Pegasus's. Then, with her dogs at her heels, she raced back to the Academy to reveal the news of Erebus's return.

12

Help!

BACK AT ECHIDNA'S CAVE, NYX HAD NO IDEA how much time had passed since she'd first landed in the rain. At least a couple of days, she guessed. L-o-n-g days since the nights were missing due to her imprisonment. Except to nab the occasional prey that wandered by the cave, Echidna had barely moved the whole time.

Nyx paced the cave, back and forth, munching

her last Hotter than Hades spicy nut bar. Since that monster slept with one eye open, she'd had no chance to try to squeeze past it and escape. What must everyone be thinking had happened to her? For sure they would've noticed her absence from the sky. *But would they even care?* she wondered with gloomy self-pity.

Maybe Echidna was right and Nyx had overestimated her importance. As that monster mommy delighted in pointing out (over and over again!), many mortals and immortals (including Zeus, though the monster didn't know it) were afraid of the dark. Maybe they would greet the endless days with rejoicing.

But what of the Oneiroi? Everyone would still need sleep somehow, sometime. Were those Dream Brothers continuing to make mischief with their

vivid dreams and nightmares, disturbing everyone's slumber at MOA? They needed to be captured and returned to the Underworld before they drove the immortals crazy! Yet here Nyx was, stuck in a cave, with no way to warn Zeus or do anything to help.

There was a flurry of sudden movement at the entrance to the cave. Some hapless animal squealed as it was caught in Echidna's horrid embrace. Next came the by-now-familiar sound of crunching bones as the monster devoured its prey.

Nyx tried to tune out the sound. "I'm so sorry I got us stuck in here," she whispered to Hypnos. Kneeling by his cage, she poked her fingers through the bars to stroke his feathers. Though her parakeet couldn't actually understand her, she added, "Love you, tweety-pie. Wish I had taken better care of you and Thanatos."

The cave was so dark that Hypnos had stayed quiet thus far, only scrabbling at the bottom of his cage occasionally to eat the birdseed she would replenish from the sack she'd packed in her black bag. Echidna seemed unaware of the bird's presence, thankfully. As prey, Hypnos would be worth little to the monster, of course. A mere crumb. But Nyx had no doubt that wouldn't stop Echidna from eating him, if only to spite Nyx. The creature was *that* cruel.

Nyx herself had eaten little since becoming trapped here. Even so, with her last Hotter than Hades bar gone now, plus most of what had been in the snack bag Artemis had given her, there was little left to eat. Not that it made any difference, she thought ruefully. It seemed only a matter of time until Echidna decided to gobble *her*.

BURP! "Mmm. *That* was yummers," boomed

her captor after its meal. "Hunting has never been so easy, little goddess of the not-night. With you around, I won't ever have to leave my cave again!"

In a taunting voice, the she-monster added, "I bet Zeus and all the other immortals are enjoying this never-ending day as much as I am. In fact, they're probably dancing around at the top of Mount Olympus to celebrate their good luck. If they only knew the favor I've done them, they'd probably put a statue of me in one of their temples!"

"Only if they wanted to scare away all visitors," Nyx muttered under her breath in a voice too low for Echidna to hear. On the other hand, the monster would probably be pleased to think that a mere statue of her could inspire fear.

Suddenly Nyx heard a familiar chirping. It was coming from somewhere outside the cave. She leaped

to her feet. Could it be? It sounded like . . . *Thanatos!* A rush of joy filled her. Somehow the bird had found them! Perhaps he had spotted Nyx's chariot while flying overhead and recognized it? He'd ridden in it often enough.

Hearing the chirping, Hypnos grew restless. He began to rattle the bars of his cage with his beak. "Shh," whispered Nyx. But her warning did no good. Despite the dark, Hypnos broke his silence. In response to Thanatos's chirping, he sang out a lovely lullaby.

In horror, Nyx saw the she-monster, framed in the opening of the cave, cock its head. "Is there a bird in here?" Echidna asked in surprise.

"Of course not," Nyx lied. "It must be an echo you hear from a bird outside in a tree." Clutching Hypnos's cage to her chest, she whispered, "Hush.

Please hush." But the parakeet kept on singing, pausing between notes to rattle the bars of his cage. Nyx tried singing even louder to drown him out, but Echidna wasn't fooled.

Suddenly, the monster's serpent tail uncoiled. The tip of it hurtled toward Nyx. It slipped around the cage and yanked it from her grasp.

Nyx gasped, guessing what was coming. "Nooo! Please!" she cried out. "He's all feathers and tiny bones. He won't make a good snack! You might even choke on him!"

The monster laughed. "Keeping him a secret from Echidna, were you?" It brought the cage up to its face to better see the parakeet. For a few moments Hypnos clammed up. Perhaps he was dizzy from being jerked around. Or maybe the sight of the monster had scared the song right out of him. But then,

hearing Thanatos's trilling outside the cave, Hypnos started up again.

"Pretty little thing, isn't it?" Echidna said, staring at Hypnos with a look of wonder. "Such a sweet voice, too." The monster mommy's mouth opened wide. Nyx gasped, fearing that Hypnos was about to be devoured, cage and all. However, Echidna only yawned sleepily. "Echidna's eyes feel so heavy. Echidna can hardly keep them open."

Though it shouldn't have surprised her, Nyx could scarcely believe it. Her bird's song was putting this monster to sleep!

Hugging the cage, the she-monster coiled its tail around itself. "Maybe I'll"—yawn—"keep him." It was the last thing the monster said before its eyelids closed and its head dropped onto its coiled tail. It began snoring away. With *both* eyes shut.

As soon as Nyx judged it was safe, she crept nearer. Experimentally, she poked Echidna's tail and then leaped back. But when the monster failed to wake, she bravely climbed its coils. Not daring to pull the birdcage from Echidna's grasp, Nyx carefully slid open its gate. Hypnos immediately flew from the cage and out the cave's opening to join Thanatos. Both birds chirped excitedly, obviously thrilled to be reunited.

Score! Nyx scrambled back down the scaly coils, knowing that Echidna could wake at any moment. As she leaped to the floor of the cave, the monster's eyes fluttered open. Nyx froze in fright.

But then Echidna's eyes merely closed again. "Me? Go on a date with you, Geryon?" the monstrous creature mumbled. "Why, I'd love to . . ." *Snuffle . . . burble . . . snore.*

Nyx almost grinned. Echidna was dreaming! She

wondered which one of the Oneiroi was responsible for the Geryon dream. Probably Phantasus, since he specialized in illusions. The idea that anyone would want to date Echidna—even a Geryon—*had* to be an illusion. Thinking about the Oneiroi reminded Nyx that they were still loose at MOA. She had to get back there!

Leaving the cage behind, Nyx grabbed her sparkly black bag. After slipping its handles over one arm, she squeezed around the snoring Echidna and raced from the cave as fast as she could.

She slowed as she came to her chariot. Too bad she couldn't use it to escape, but it was useless without her horse to pull it. "Where, oh where, are you, Erebus?" she murmured, knowing there'd be no reply. If only she could snap her fingers and make him appear! But that couldn't happen since she'd

never snapped him away in the first place. This was simply how his magic worked.

Both of her birds fluttered down from the tree they'd been perching in to follow her as she sprinted off through the woods, leaving the chariot behind. "I'm so happy you're okay, Thanatos!" she called up in delight as she continued to put as much distance as possible between herself and the cave. Noticing how plump the green-and-yellow parakeet was looking, she smiled. "Good bird! Looks like you found plenty to eat while you were on your own, didn't you?" Thanatos chirped happily at her.

Suddenly, an ear-shattering screech split the air. "Uh-oh, I think Echidna woke up!" Nyx exclaimed to her pets. "Fly!" she shouted. As they took off higher into the sky above her, she followed as best she could, zooming across the forest floor.

Screaming curses, the monster slithered after her, bellowing, "Echidna *will* catch you, little goddess. And then Echidna will swallow you whole!"

Nyx ran so fast she felt like her lungs were on fire. Still, the slithering sounds came closer and the monster's screeches grew louder. It was catching up!

Ar-rooo! Ar-ooo! All at once Nyx heard the sound of baying hounds. Her heart skipped a beat. *Artemis's dogs!* And they weren't far away! A minute or two later all three dogs were upon her, leaping to lick her hands and face.

Happy as Nyx was to see them, she was suddenly scared for them as well. She'd seen what Echidna did to the prey she caught, and Artemis's hounds would be no match for the monster. She pushed the dogs off her. "Run!" she yelled. As if sensing her fright, they obeyed. But though they bounded ahead of her, they turned their heads every now and again as if to make sure she was following.

Huffing and puffing, Nyx kept on going. Only she was running out of steam. Daring to glance over her shoulder, she saw that Echidna was right behind her. Suddenly the monster's tail lashed out. "Gotcha!" it yelled. Its tail coiled around Nyx's waist.

As she was lifted into the air, Nyx squeezed her eyes shut. She knew this was the end!

13

Happy Surprises

JUST THEN NYX HEARD A WHINNY. *EREBUS?* HER eyes popped open. She looked up, and there he was high in the sky above her. And he was pulling an MOA chariot with Artemis at the reins! As the chariot swooped toward Nyx, she saw that Persephone, Athena, and Aphrodite were on board. The latter two girls reached down to her, yelling, "Grab on!"

Nyx swung her bag up to them. Then she grabbed

their hands and they yanked her free of Echidna's coiled tail. With perfect timing, Artemis expertly whipped the chariot higher, safely beyond Echidna's reach.

"Come back here, lunch!" the monster screamed angrily.

"As if!" Artemis yelled down at Echidna. Then she grinned over at Nyx, and the girls all laughed. Far below, the grumpy monster shook its fist.

"Thanks for the rescue!" said Nyx. Aphrodite and Athena had deposited her in the backseat between them, and now she tried to catch her breath as the chariot sailed upward.

From the front seat, Persephone looked over her shoulder at Nyx. "Yeah, looks like we got here in the nick of time."

Nyx nodded gravely. "You can say that again."

"Hey, aren't those your birds?" Aphrodite asked Nyx. She pointed to two parakeets flying just above and ahead of them.

"You found Thanatos!" Artemis noted gleefully.

"No, he found me!" said Nyx, her heart lifting at the sight of her birds. Erebus had spotted the parakeets too, and gave a joyful whinny. Hearing him, the two birds circled down to land on his head, clinging to his fluffy mane.

Spotting her hounds down below, Artemis swooped to pick them up too. "Just in case Echidna decides to come after them," she commented. Once on board, Suez and Nectar settled at Artemis's feet, while Amby sat in Persephone's lap. As the chariot rose again and the wind whistled past it, the beagle's long floppy ears streamed behind him. Soon Nyx's parakeets fluttered over to land on her shoulder.

Fortunately, the tired dogs ignored them.

While Artemis guided the chariot back to MOA, Nyx told the four goddessgirls the story of how she'd come to be holed up in Echidna's cave and how she'd finally managed to escape when her birds' singing caused the monster to fall deeply asleep . . . for a short time, anyway. She also explained her theory about Thanatos finding her because he'd spotted her chariot. "Too bad I had to leave it behind. But I'm glad Erebus escaped, or you might never have known something was wrong."

Artemis cleared her throat. "Speaking of something wrong," she said, shooting Nyx a strange look over her shoulder. "It's been a crazy few days since you left. Remember those shadows I thought I saw flitting from your bag that first day you arrived?"

"The Oneiroi!" Nyx exclaimed. She pulled Eos's

notescroll from her pocket and read it aloud to the other girls. "I feel so stupid for not realizing they'd followed me to MOA," she admitted to Artemis. "And for thinking you'd only imagined you'd seen something."

"S'okay," said Artemis, sounding oddly relieved. "We all make mistakes."

"Not me," quipped Aphrodite. "I'm perfect." Which made them all laugh.

Puzzling over the note of relief she'd heard in Artemis's voice, Nyx hoped these girls hadn't suspected her of *deliberately* bringing the Oneiroi to MOA!

"When we left this morning to come find you, Zeus and Hades and a bunch of other students and teachers at MOA were out searching for the Oneiroi," Persephone informed Nyx. Then she explained how she and Hades had gone looking for Nyx in the

Underworld when night failed to come and how the real Hypnos and Thanatos had told them that the Oneiroi were missing. "Hades says they're not going to be easy to capture."

"Especially with everyone being so cranky and not thinking clearly due to lack of sleep lately," Aphrodite remarked. She had coaxed Hypnos to fly to her palm and was stroking the bird's feathers. "The combination of continual daylight and all the Oneiroi-inspired dreams and nightmares has done everyone in."

"Dad and Hera are more tired than ever," Athena added with a sigh. "Hebe seems to sense there's no night and stays awake even if the curtains are closed against the sun. Everyone's been making blackout curtains to hang over their windows, which helps some people sleep at least."

"Yeah, but MOA is starting to feel as closed in and dark as a tomb," Artemis said.

Nyx felt her chest tighten with worry. "I guess Zeus is even madder at me now than he was before."

There was an uncertain silence. Then Athena hastened to reassure her. "He'll calm down when we explain what happened."

But having seen Zeus lose his temper, Nyx was not comforted.

Their chariot was about halfway up Mount Olympus, passing above the Immortal Marketplace, when Nyx's two parakeets suddenly flew off! The girls craned their necks to follow their path. "They're making a beeline for the IM!" said Athena.

The birds sailed over the glass-ceilinged marketplace till they came to an open skylight. Then they dove through it. "That skylight leads into the Ship

Shape pet shop!" Persephone exclaimed.

"We have to follow them. I'm so sorry!" Nyx apologized. "They probably heard other birds chirping in there and wanted to join them for a while."

"So we'll take a little detour. It's fine," Artemis assured her. After circling the skylight, she landed the MOA chariot at the marketplace entrance closest to the shop. Nyx slung her sparkly black bag over one shoulder.

As she and the others got down from the chariot, she wondered what she should do about Erebus. Normally, she'd snap him away until her return. However, when he'd bolted from beside Echidna's cave he might have damaged the magical link between him and the chariot that allowed her to move them as a pair. Who knew where her snap might send him now? She definitely didn't want to chance sending him back to the chariot and into that monster's clutches again!

She was relieved when she turned to find Artemis still seated aboard the MOA chariot. "I'll wait here and keep my dogs and your horse company," she announced.

Nyx smiled in appreciation. "Thanks."

She and the other three goddessgirls headed into the marketplace. Once inside, Aphrodite suggested, "Why don't you go with Nyx to the pet store, Athena? Persephone and I will go to Hermes' Delivery kiosk and send a message ahead to MOA about finding Nyx and to explain where she's been."

"Good idea," said Athena. "Let's meet back at the chariot as soon as we're all done."

The girls split up outside a shop called Magical Wagical, which was right next to a blue door that

marked the entrance to Ship Shape. As the other two girls headed for Hermes' Delivery kiosk, Nyx and Athena pushed through the blue door. Then they made their way up a gangplank that rested on pontoons atop a lake. The whole inside of the shop was a big freshwater pool! All kinds of fish frolicked around in the lake, and birds flew in and out of the shop through the open skylight in the ceiling.

"Look, there they are!" Nyx exclaimed to Athena, pointing. Her parakeets were at the far end of the gangplank where it joined up with the wooden sailing ship where things were for sale. Both were perched together on one of the thick rope handrails that ran along either side of the gangplank.

Seeing Nyx, Hypnos let out a chirp and both birds fluttered over to land on one of her shoulders.

"Good boys," Nyx cooed to them, since they hadn't really meant to cause trouble.

Nyx looked at Athena. "I know we're in a hurry, but do you think I could go in the ship and buy a new cage and more seed for my parakeets?"

"Sure," said Athena.

The girls had to stoop to duck through the small open hatch door that led into the ship. The walls inside it were lined with shelves stocked with bags of birdseed, boxes of fish food, and various other things for birds and fish, including cages and aquariums.

A man wearing an orange-feathered tunic came toward the two girls. He had blue-green hair that stood up in a straight ruff from his forehead to the back of his neck like a Mohawk haircut. A name tag pinned to his tunic read, CEYX KINGFISHER, CO-OWNER. Tilting his head sideways in a curiously birdlike fashion, he angled one of his eyes to look first at Nyx and then at Athena. "May I help you?" he asked.

"Yes, please. I need a bag of seed for my two parakeets, and a new cage, too," said Nyx.

"Would you like to try some of our new no-mess seed?" the man asked her. "It's had a spell cast over it so that birds can't toss it out of their food dish all over the bottom of the cage or onto the floor. Makes clean-up a breeze."

"Yes, thanks," said Nyx. "Sounds great!"

As the man was getting the seed from a shelf, a woman appeared from a back room. She was also dressed in an orange-feathered tunic and had a blue-green Mohawk haircut. "Did I hear you say you needed a new birdcage?" she asked, tilting her head to look at Nyx in the same birdlike way the man had. Her name tag read ALCYONE KINGFISHER, CO-OWNER.

Nyx guessed the pair were probably husband and wife. "That's right," she said. "Their old one got, um, *lost*."

Athena had already begun to examine the various cages on a shelf against one of the walls. "How about this one, Nyx?" she said, holding up a beautiful cylindrical gold cage with a peaked top and long vertical bars spaced about a half inch apart. A design of metallic copper poppies was melded to the bars on the lower third of the cage.

As Nyx gave her a thumbs-up, Alcyone made another birdlike turn of her head. Regarding Nyx through her opposite eye, she said in surprise, "You're Nyx? Goddess of the night?"

Nyx nodded.

"Ceyx!" Alcyone exclaimed to the man as he came up to them with the seed. "It's *her*! The missing goddessgirl we read about in the *Greekly Weekly*." Both birds tilted their heads and eyed Nyx again.

"Where have you been?" demanded Ceyx.

"We heard you fell in love with that actor, Orion," Alcyone went on. "And then turned yourself into a star so you could hang out with him, not realizing he wasn't actually a star in the sky, but the other kind of star instead."

Nyx blushed. Did people think she was too dumb to know the difference between a star in the sky and the actor kind of star? Besides, she'd never even *met* Orion. And what little she knew about him from articles in *Teen Scrollazine* made him sound pretty full of himself, not at all the kind of boy she would like. "Um . . . it's a long story," she replied.

"One we don't have time for right now," Athena added as she lifted down the gold birdcage. Alcyone hurried to take it from her, then rang up both the cage and the bag of birdseed at the store's sales counter.

Suddenly glad she hadn't thought to leave her travel bag with Artemis, Nyx pulled her coin purse from it and handed Alcyone enough drachmas to pay for her purchases. Good thing she'd packed some money to bring after all! "The rumor you heard isn't true, by the way," she told Alcyone. "I'm sorry I haven't been around, but I promise I'll be back at work tonight as usual."

"That's a relief," said Ceyx, coming to stand behind the counter too. "This endless daylight is for the birds."

"But even we . . . I mean *they* don't care for it," Alcyone chirped. Nyx smiled at her slip of the tongue. Judging from the appearance and mannerisms of the shop owners, she guessed they must be shape-shifters. Which meant that they could switch back and forth between their human and bird forms.

"Would you like a cover, too?" asked Ceyx. "Comes with the cage," he added as Nyx peered into her nearly empty coin purse.

"Sure, thanks." The cover for her old birdcage was somewhere in her bag, but it wouldn't have fit this new cage in any case. The new one was taller than the other cage had been.

Nyx put the seed and the new cage cover into her black bag and looped the bag's handles over her arm. Then, as Ceyx held the cage's gate open for her, she gently moved her birds from her shoulder into their new home. "What are their names?" the shopkeeper asked as the parakeets fluttered around inside their cage, checking it out.

Athena shifted from one foot to the other. Nyx could tell that the goddessgirl was impatient to be off. Nyx was, too, but she didn't want to be impolite. Besides, she liked talking about her pets with other pet lovers.

"Hypnos is the blue-and-white bird," Nyx said. "The other is Thanatos. I got them as a gift from a shade. He couldn't keep them because shades aren't allowed any live pets in the Underworld. But I'm immortal, of course. I named them after two brothers that are friends of mine." With that, she lifted the cage down from the counter and turned to go.

"Two brothers?" Ceyx repeated. Hearing the sharp surprise in his voice, Nyx stopped in her tracks and turned back. The pair of shopkeepers tilted their heads and exchanged a look.

"Actually, the green-and-yellow bird, the one you call Thanatos, is a female," Ceyx informed Nyx.

"The clue is the band of raised skin across the top of her beak where her nostrils are," he said, pointing. "That's called the *cere*. Girl parakeets normally have pinkish-brown ceres, and boy parakeets usually have blue ones."

"And judging from the look of your girl, she's going to lay eggs soon," Alcyone added.

"Ye gods, how cool!" exclaimed Athena.

Nyx's eyes widened in astonishment. Grinning at Athena, she said, "Guess I should've known. I *did* notice that Thanatos was looking fatter!" The happy and unexpected news that he . . . er . . . *she* . . . was about to have some babies helped to lessen the embarrassment Nyx felt for not having realized that her parakeets were male and female. "Thanks for everything!" she told the shopkeepers. Then the two girls dashed off.

14

Caught!

WHEN NYX AND ATHENA GOT BACK TO THE chariot, they found Artemis, Aphrodite, and Persephone waiting for them. Erebus had been grazing nearby and the dogs were frolicking in the grass, but now Artemis harnessed the horse and herded her dogs into the chariot. Hypnos and Thanatos fluttered around inside their new birdcage as Nyx handed it up to Aphrodite before climbing in to sit in back with her and Athena again.

"Pretty cage," Aphrodite commented as Erebus quickly whisked the chariot skyward. "I like the poppy design."

When the other goddessgirls laughed, Nyx wasn't sure what to think. "Did I miss a joke?" she asked.

Aphrodite grinned. "They're laughing because they remember a bag I once had. It had a poppy design on it too. But it wasn't a tasteful design like these copper poppies. No, my purse poppies were big, floppy, and yellow. Buying that bag was a fashion mistake," she admitted cheerfully.

"A mistake we're determined you'll never live down," Persephone teased fondly.

It was good to know that even the goddessgirl of love and beauty could make the occasional fashion error. Aphrodite's easygoing confession led to Nyx's own. She gave Athena a smile and then said to the other three girls, "Guess what? Thanatos is a girl, not a boy! Not only that, she's going to be a mama bird soon!"

After the girls expressed their surprise and delight at the news, Nyx explained what she'd learned at Ship Shape about the different color ceres for male and female parakeets. "Come to think of it," she added, "I probably missed a clue that my birds were nesting." She explained about the papyrus sheets she always stacked at the bottom of the cage to catch spilled seed and droppings. "When I was cleaning their old cage last Monday, I saw that some of the papyrus had been torn and chewed into a little pile."

Persephone grinned. "I bet you're right. They were probably starting to build a nest of papyrus shavings!"

Holding Erebus's reins in a slack grip, Artemis glanced over her shoulder. "Think maybe Thanatos discovered the loose bar in their cage when he, um, *she* was building her nest?"

"Yeah, could be," Nyx agreed. But soon she grew quiet, having spotted a hint of Mount Olympus Academy up ahead.

The chariot had barely touched down at the far side of MOA's courtyard when Hades came running up. He flipped a lock of curly dark hair out of his eyes and grinned at Nyx. "Hey! Glad you're back!"

"Thanks," she replied. She hoped others here would feel the same.

Artemis's dogs leaped down from the chariot and the girls followed suit. As the dogs raced ahead to the Academy, Nyx kissed Erebus on the nose. "You helped save me today, buddy," she told him softly.

"Thank you." Then she admitted her concerns to the others about what might happen if she tried to snap Erebus away now that the connection between him and the magical chariot was likely damaged.

"The chariot might disappear too, and then rejoin with Erebus the next time I snapped him into being," Nyx said. "But I can't count on that. What if the magic pulls Erebus back to where the chariot is standing next to Echidna's cave, instead?" She shuddered.

"Best to leave him be for now, then," said Artemis. "Why don't I take him to the stable while you go on ahead with the others."

Nyx gratefully took her up on her offer. She needed to find out what was happening with the Oneiroi! Aphrodite passed Nyx her birdcage, but Athena carried her bag as the girls and Hades began to walk toward the Academy. "Zeus told me about the message you all sent from the IM while we were chasing after the Oneiroi," he informed the girls.

Had he and Zeus caught the Oneiroi, then? Before Nyx could ask, Hades glanced over at her and said, "Being trapped in a cave with Echidna was probably no picnic."

"Too true," Nyx agreed. Then she grinned. "As a matter of fact, I almost *was* the picnic!" She could joke about her terror now that the true danger had passed!

The others laughed. Nyx was pleased with herself. After only days here at MOA, she'd gotten pretty good at joking around. It definitely helped that these goddessgirls had been so nice to her. It seemed that her friendly side had been asleep and had only needed awakening through use.

Persephone joined hands with her crush. Then she asked Hades the same question Nyx had been planning to ask. "Did you catch any of those Oneiroi?"

"I didn't know it at the time," Nyx explained to him hastily, "but they hitched a ride in my chariot when I first came here."

Hades nodded. "I figured as much." Then he frowned. "Zeus and I almost had those ornery Oneiroi cornered a few minutes ago, but they gave us the slip. They'd be easier to corral if they weren't so foglike and didn't zip around so fast. Not to mention the fact that they can squeeze through openings as small as an inch wide."

"Any idea where they are now?" Nyx asked as they crossed the marble courtyard. She noticed Apollo had gathered Artemis's dogs and was taking them off for a walk, probably so they wouldn't get in the way of efforts to capture the Oneiroi.

"Somewhere in there," Hades replied, gesturing up at the Academy building. A half-dozen students stood outside its front doors holding nets at the ready. "We closed all the windows so the Oneiroi couldn't escape, and a bunch of us have been watching the front doors as people go in and out. If the Oneiroi do manage to escape, we're hoping those nets will capture them."

Hades opened the doors and the group darted inside the Academy. The students on guard quickly closed the doors behind them. There were dozens more students inside the entryway and nearby halls, searching nooks and crannies for the troublemaking trio of brothers.

Up till now, Hypnos and Thanatos had been

fairly quiet even though their cage was uncovered. However, upon the sudden dash inside, they began to chirp. Glancing down at them as they cuddled together in their shiny gold cage, Nyx got an idea.

Taking her bag from Athena, she drew out her folded cape. Then she slid open the gate to her birds' cage and coaxed the pair out. Singing cheerfully, they flew up to the domed ceiling. A ring of eight ionic columns supported the ceiling, and the birds perched at the top of one of those columns on the scrolled capital.

Of course, Hypnos's and Thanatos's singing echoed throughout the Academy, thus making Nyx (as well as everyone else!) drowsy. She forced herself to stay wide awake and noticed others doing the same. They were blinking and trying not to yawn as they all gazed upward.

Screee! Screee!

Students began covering their ears. "What's that awful sound?"

"Make it stop!"

"There! Look! They're singing too!" yelled Nyx, pointing at three shadowy figures up near the ceiling. She smiled to herself. Just like at home in the Underworld, Hypnos's and Thanatos's singing had drawn the spirits near.

"The Oneiroi!" shouted Hades.

Nyx whistled to her birds. Still singing, they left their perch and flew down to her shoulder. Mesmerized by their song, the screeching spirits floated downward too. They wove in and out of each other, seeming to combine as one shadow at times before separating again.

As soon as they drew close enough, Nyx whipped her cape outward. It ballooned up and then floated

down to settle over all three Oneiroi. Expertly tugging on the cape, she reeled them in. Once her cape had shrunk to about the size of a pillowcase, she bunched its edges up tight in her fists.

"You bagged 'em!" shouted Artemis, who'd arrived back from the stable just in time to see the capture. Angry at their confinement, the Oneiroi flapped wildly inside the cape, trying to get free.

"Bring the birdcage!" yelled Nyx. Athena was closest to it and so rushed it over to her as instructed. Guessing Nyx's intention, Athena opened the gate while Nyx thrust her bunched cape up to it. Everyone held their breath as she loosened her hands . . . just enough. Three wispy shadows flew out of the cape—and into the cage! Quickly, Nyx withdrew her cape. Athena slammed the gate shut and Artemis fastened its clasp. *Gotcha!*

"Since the cage bars are no more than a half inch apart, the Oneiroi should stay trapped," Hades crowed gleefully.

To make double sure they couldn't escape, Nyx brought out the cover the shopkeepers had given her. While she refolded her cape, Persephone found the old cord and Aphrodite wrapped it around the cover before knotting it tightly.

Just then Zeus stormed into the entryway. Electricity crackled up and down his muscled arms as his eyes darted from student to student. "You!" he boomed, singling out Nyx with a pointed finger.

Nyx froze in terror. Hypnos must have remembered Zeus (and his thunderbolts) only *too* well. He gave a loud squawk and zoomed up to the dome again. Meanwhile Thanatos cowered close to Nyx's neck, hiding under her hair.

Before Zeus could speak further, Athena said, "Isn't it great, Dad? Nyx's birds lured the Oneiroi down, and she imprisoned the spirits in her bird-cage!" Several students pointed to the cage, drawing Zeus's gaze.

"Huh?" Zeus's blazing blue eyes narrowed. Students backed away as he went to the cage and thumped it.

On cue, the Oneiroi renewed their high-pitched squeals. Only this time, they were probably protesting their captivity rather than trying to sing!

Instantly, Zeus's demeanor changed. "Well done!" he thundered, beaming happily at Nyx. Glancing around, he pointed at the four girls who'd rescued her from Echidna. "Get to my office, you four! You too, Hades! And Nyx!" Then he whirled around and led the way there himself.

Nyx picked up the birdcage—now a temporary prison for the Oneiroi—and started to follow along with the others. Perhaps sensing that Zeus no longer meant him any harm, Hypnos flew down again. He landed on top of the principal's head! Nyx gasped, but Zeus only laughed and reached up gently to transfer Hypnos to one of his fingers.

"No sneezing," Athena murmured to Nyx as they walked. "That's a good sign. I guess Dad's not allergic to birds."

When the students entered the principal's office, Nyx was happily surprised at how hospitable he became. He dragged an overstuffed chair covered in the same blue-and-gold-striped fabric as the cushions on his other chairs close to his throne. "You can sit here," he told her. "It's my most comfortable visitor's chair." He even brushed the chip bag and baby toys off the seat of it before she sat down.

"Set the cage on my desk for now, where we can all keep an eye on it," Zeus suggested. "Just in case."

As Nyx did that, Athena, Artemis, Aphrodite, Persephone, and Hades took (slightly less comfortable) chairs nearby. Still holding Hypnos on his outstretched finger, Zeus lowered himself onto the golden throne behind his huge desk. "Ahem," he said, clearing his throat. "I think perhaps I was a little hasty in asking you to leave MOA, Nyx."

She blinked. He'd been *asking* her to leave? She'd hate to think what he sounded like when he was giving *orders*! But no matter. At least he didn't seem angry now. In fact, Zeus had begun to gently stroke Hypnos's feathered back with his finger. Suddenly Thanatos sidestepped out from behind Nyx's hair and flew toward him. Zeus gave a hearty laugh as

Thanatos landed beside Hypnos on his finger. Looking at the two birds, he said, "It seems you two feathered friends are heroes."

On the way to Zeus's office the Oneiroi's high-pitched squeals had quieted, but now they started up again and grew even louder. And the cover over the cage began to poke out in places as the spirited trio lashed at the bars of the cage. Zeus looked over at Hades. "Can you find a more suitable container for them?"

Hades leaped up. "I have an urn in my room that'll work. I can take them back to the Underworld after I transfer them to it."

"Perfect," said Zeus. As the godboy dashed off with the cage, Zeus glanced over at Athena and her BFFs. "Good work rescuing Nyx and sending me that notescroll to keep me informed," he praised.

Then he turned back to Nyx again. "How are you feeling after your encounter with Echidna?" he asked sympathetically.

"Fine," Nyx assured him. She smiled around at the other girls. "Thanks to them."

"Excellent," said Zeus. There was a pause and he squirmed in his throne a bit. "Ahem . . . I don't suppose . . . um . . . that you might be ready to return to the sky tonight?" he said at last. "You see, I've been getting a lot of flak from everyone—mortals and immortals alike. Seems they miss the rest and calm that your darkness brings."

Athena leaned forward in her chair. "And how about you, Dad?" she dared to ask. "Do you miss the night too?"

Caught off guard, Zeus squirmed some more, then mumbled, "Well, I . . . um . . . yes, I do." Looking down

at the birds on his finger, he murmured, "Who knew night was so necessary to balance day! Day is all very light and bright, but night is best for rest." His face brightened. "Hey, that rhymes!"

Nyx grinned. She wondered if Zeus would still sleep with his lighted winged-horse lamp in spite of his new understanding of night. That would be cool with her, of course. Everyone had fears. She herself was afraid of spiders, though she knew most of them were beneficial and couldn't hurt her. One could understand the value of something despite having an irrational fear of it, she decided.

Sitting across from Zeus, she noticed that the dark circles under his eyes were darker than the first time she'd seen him. And his hair was wilder than ever. Like everyone else, he must've gotten very little sleep these last few days and was as tired as the rest of them. "I'm fine now," she repeated. "And ready to return to work."

"Only, her chariot is still back at Echidna's cave," Persephone noted.

"And she really needs it," added Artemis. "Her horse and her chariot are a matched magical pair!"

"You can borrow one of the school's chariots for tonight," Zeus told Nyx eagerly. "We don't want to delay you another night, no sir. In the morning I can send a certain hundred-eyed giant named Argus Panoptes, a devoted friend of Hera's, to retrieve your chariot and deliver it here to MOA." He smiled at the birds again. "And if Echidna isn't happy to give up the chariot, Argus will *persuade* her."

"Thank you," said Nyx. What a relief it was to know she'd get her chariot back. Once it was hooked up to Erebus again, Nyx was sure their

magical connection would be restored.

"And so can Nyx stay at MOA the rest of the week as planned?" pressed Aphrodite.

"Yes, of course!" Zeus agreed readily. He spread his muscled arms wide, in a generous, jolly mood now. "Stay as long as you want, Nyx."

Artemis smiled at Nyx. "I've been thinking," she said, glancing around at the group. "To celebrate Nyx's importance as a goddess, I'd like to put a statue of her in my temple in Ephesus. To sort of sing the praises of an unsung hero in an official way."

Nyx's jaw dropped. She stared at the goddessgirl, hardly able to believe that she would do something so nice for her. This seemed proof that Artemis saw her as a special friend just as Nyx did her. How cool was that? she thought happily.

"Great idea, Dad!" Athena said enthusiastically. "In

fact, I bet you had the same idea. It's just that Artemis said it first."

That clever Athena, Nyx thought with admiration. It was common knowledge that Zeus liked to think all good ideas were his own. And Artemis probably needed his approval on the statue, even if it was for her own temple.

"Well . . . I . . . ," he started to say. But before he could come to a decision, Hades was back.

"Got 'em!" he announced. He carried a stoppered clay jar under one arm and was clutching the empty birdcage in his other arm.

Nyx sprang from her chair to meet him. "Thanks," she said, taking the cage.

"Sure thing," Hades replied. "Thanks again for catching the Dream Team! See you around the Underworld!" He waved to Zeus and the other girls.

"Later!" Then he was off with the clay urn to return the Oneiroi to their home in Tartarus.

"Well, that settles that," Zeus said in relief. "Everyone's dreams should be a bit more subdued with those three pesky sleep-wrecking brothers back where they belong." Saying nothing about the statue, he stood from his desk and carried Hypnos and Thanatos over to Nyx. As she opened the gate to their cage and Zeus bent to lower the birds inside, she wondered if he had already forgotten about Artemis's idea.

After the birds fluttered to the swing that hung from the top of the cage, Zeus straightened and turned back to his throne. "That will be all, girls."

Understanding that this was their cue to leave, they all leaped up from their chairs. But at the door, Athena paused to look over her shoulder at her dad, who had kicked back and crossed his feet on top of his desk. "About what Artemis suggested before . . ."

Zeus's answer was immediate this time. "What? Oh yes, by all means." He smiled at Nyx. "For all you do *night* in and *night* out, you deserve to be a *sung* hero, not just an unsung one." As if voicing their agreement, Nyx's birds began to chirp.

A warm feeling washed over Nyx and she smiled back at Zeus. And then at Artemis and the other girls too. "Thank you so much! The statue will be such an honor!"

As soon as the girls left Zeus's office, Persephone and Aphrodite peeled off from them to run an errand. Athena and Artemis, however, went with Nyx to the cafeteria so she could grab some snacks. It was almost time for her to return night to the world.

Minutes later Nyx was out in the courtyard with

her sparkly black bag. She was surprised to find a crowd of students waiting for her. It seemed that Persephone and Aphrodite, with the help of Pheme, had been busily spreading the news of Nyx's terrifying adventure and an account (for those who hadn't witnessed it themselves) of how she and her birds had captured the Oneiroi on her return to MOA.

Now all the students applauded and cheered her. Even Poseidon. "Hooray for Nyx, goddess of the night!" they all shouted. Their response to her return to MOA was certainly different from the way they'd stared at her on her arrival last Sunday!

Nyx beamed. She, and above all, the importance of the night she created, were better understood now. Maybe even prized!

After leaving her birds in Artemis's care, leading Erebus from the stable, and donning her starry cape, she was soon away in one of the school's chariots. She waved down at the students for as long as she could see them. As her cape's darkness settled over the weary world like a soft black blanket, every living thing seemed to sigh with relief.

Mere words had not been enough to convince others of the value of night, she realized. Instead, they'd had to *experience* what it was like to go without darkness to truly understand their need for it. She remembered what Zeus had said in his office earlier. "Who knew night was so necessary to balance day!" Well, now maybe *everyone* knew.

As Erebus soared higher and Nyx's cape began to throw off its stars, it occurred to her that balance was important in many things, not just night and day. Take joy and sadness, for example. Wasn't her joy in Thanatos's return that much deeper after the sadness of losing him . . . er . . . *her*?

Then there was fear and courage. She had been so frightened when she was trapped in Echidna's cave. But she had kept her wits about her and discovered a bravery within herself she hadn't known she possessed. In a way, that made being trapped in Echidna's cave almost worthwhile. Though it wasn't an experience she'd care to repeat, mind you!

While watching for the constellations to appear, she thought about the balance between time alone and time spent with others. She'd always thought of herself as a loner. And she'd been fine with that. However, although she valued her time alone, her experience at MOA had changed her. From now on she would seek out more opportunities for friendships, she decided. And she would keep in touch with Artemis and her BFFs and the other new friends she'd made at MOA.

Soon the sisters that composed the Hyades began to twinkle in their usual positions high in the sky. Nyx's heart leaped to see her star friends again. They were probably all wondering where she had been, and she had so much to tell them about her adventure of the last few days!

"Onward and upward, Erebus!" she exclaimed, giving his reins a shake. And soon they were soaring together among the glorious stars, bringing rest and comfort and all that the precious night meant, to the entire world below.

15
Night and Day

Some weeks later . . .

NIGHT WAS ENDING WHEN NYX ZOOMED PAST the goddess of the dawn. They waved to each other. "Did you have a good night?" Eos called up to Nyx.

Nyx nodded. "Yeah! Hope you have a good *day*!" They both laughed. Their friendship had been growing ever since Nyx had written a notescroll to Eos

thanking her for her kind warning about the Oneiroi.

Now the two goddessgirls often traded note-scrolls back and forth as they passed. And once Eos had even tossed Nyx a pretty speckled shell she'd found on the shores of the Aegean Sea. At home Nyx had set it on a wooden table inlaid with a mother-of-pearl design of the moon and the stars, so she could admire the shell daily. She planned to make Eos a sparkly star-shaped ornament in return very soon.

Though Nyx still enjoyed time alone, it was nice not to feel quite *so* alone anymore, to have a new friend her own age who truly understood what it was like to have a regular responsibility to the world and all who dwelled there. Their friendship would always be just a fleeting few moments during this night-to-dawn changeover, but nonetheless, it was a sweet connection.

She had just entered her palace in the Underworld when a magic breeze whisked two letterscrolls—one tied with a gold ribbon, the other with a red ribbon—through an open window. Eager as Nyx was to read them, she first tended to Hypnos and Thanatos and their four baby parakeets, now many weeks old. A fifth baby she'd sent as a gift (via Hades) to Zeus and Hera for Hebe. Nyx had noticed that the baby bird's singing was relaxing but didn't make her sleep so deeply as the songs of its parents. She named the baby bird Iremía, which means *calm*.

After she refilled her bird family's water dish and gave them more of the fabulous no-mess seed she'd bought at Ship Shape, she plopped into a chair and untied and unrolled the gold-ribboned letterscroll. It was from Hera, a thank-you note for the baby parakeet. Nyx read it aloud to her birds:

Dear Nyx,

Zeus and I can't thank you enough for your wonderful gift to Hebe. Whenever she (or we!) are feeling fussy, Iremía's cheerful singing really improves our mood.

Our little baby adores nighttime rides with Zeus on Pegasus. He never fails to point up at the starry sky and tell her, "There goes Nyx!"

Zeus says to tell you that you are welcome back at MOA anytime you'd care to visit.

Fondly,

Hera

With a smile, Nyx set aside Hera's letter. Then she slipped the red ribbon off the second scroll and unrolled it. This one was from Artemis and Athena. The *third* scroll they'd written her since she'd returned home. And each time she'd written them back, naturally. Long, newsy letterscrolls, like the ones they sent her, only about life in Tartarus, the birth and development of the baby parakeets, anecdotes about the shades, and about the antics of the *real* Hypnos and Thanatos.

Despite their eternal bickering, the two brothers were unwavering in their support of her. When she'd told them all that had happened to her while she was away—including getting kicked out of the Academy for a time—they'd insisted that Zeus had acted hastily. And they were super pleased on her behalf that he'd finally seen the light about night.

Artemis and Athena's new letter was shorter than the others the two goddessgirls had sent. Nyx read it aloud to her birds, too:

> HI, NYX,
>
> GUESS WHAT? THERE'S GOING TO BE AN UNVEILING OF A CERTAIN STATUE WE'VE ALL BEEN WAITING FOR AT ARTEMIS'S TEMPLE IN EPHESUS THIS COMING SATURDAY AT 2PM.
>
> YOU HAVE TO COME! (PLEASE, PLEASE)
>
> HADES HAS AGREED TO CHAUFFEUR YOU TO THE TEMPLE AND GET YOU BACK IN PLENTY OF TIME FOR YOU TO DO YOUR VERY IMPORTANT JOB.
>
> SEE YOU THERE! (HOPE, HOPE)

Your friends,

Artemis and Athena

P.S. Aphrodite and Persephone and lots of other students at MOA say "Hi." They love that we share your letters with them.

"Wow!" Nyx hopped up and did a happy dance, waving the scroll around. "That is so cool about the statue! And that Artemis and Athena share my letters with other MOA students, right?" she told her birds.

Saturday was the day after tomorrow, and of course she'd go. With a fingertip she traced the words "very important." They had been darkened to make them stand out. *So there, Echidna! I am too an important goddess!* she thought. She'd try not to let it go to her head, however. Still, it tickled her that she was going to get a statue when she remembered how Echidna had taunted her, saying that the gods would probably honor *her* with one if she rid the world of Nyx. Anything involving immortal temples usually made the news. Wait till that horrible she-monster heard about this!

Nyx rolled up the scrolls and set them on her wooden table beside the speckled shell Eos had given her. With a yawn she bid her birds "good day." Then she went down the hall to her bedroom.

While changing for bed she thought about how most of the world's inhabitants would be rising now and going about their day. It made her feel proud to think that because she had performed her *very important* job—and because the Oneiroi were now back where they belonged!—everyone would be well rested.

Yawning, she shoved back the heavy black brocade curtain that surrounded her bed and climbed into it. She could hear her bird family's sweet singing from down the hall. With a contented sigh, she snuggled down under the covers and soon was fast asleep.

Don't miss the next adventure in
the Goddess Girls *series!*

Coming Soon
December 2017